FACE TO FACE

Face to Face

A COLLECTION OF DRAWINGS & POLITICAL CARTOONS BY FONS VAN WOERKOM

WITH AN INTRODUCTION BY HARRISON E. SALISBURY

ALFRED A. KNOPF ✦ NEW YORK, 1973

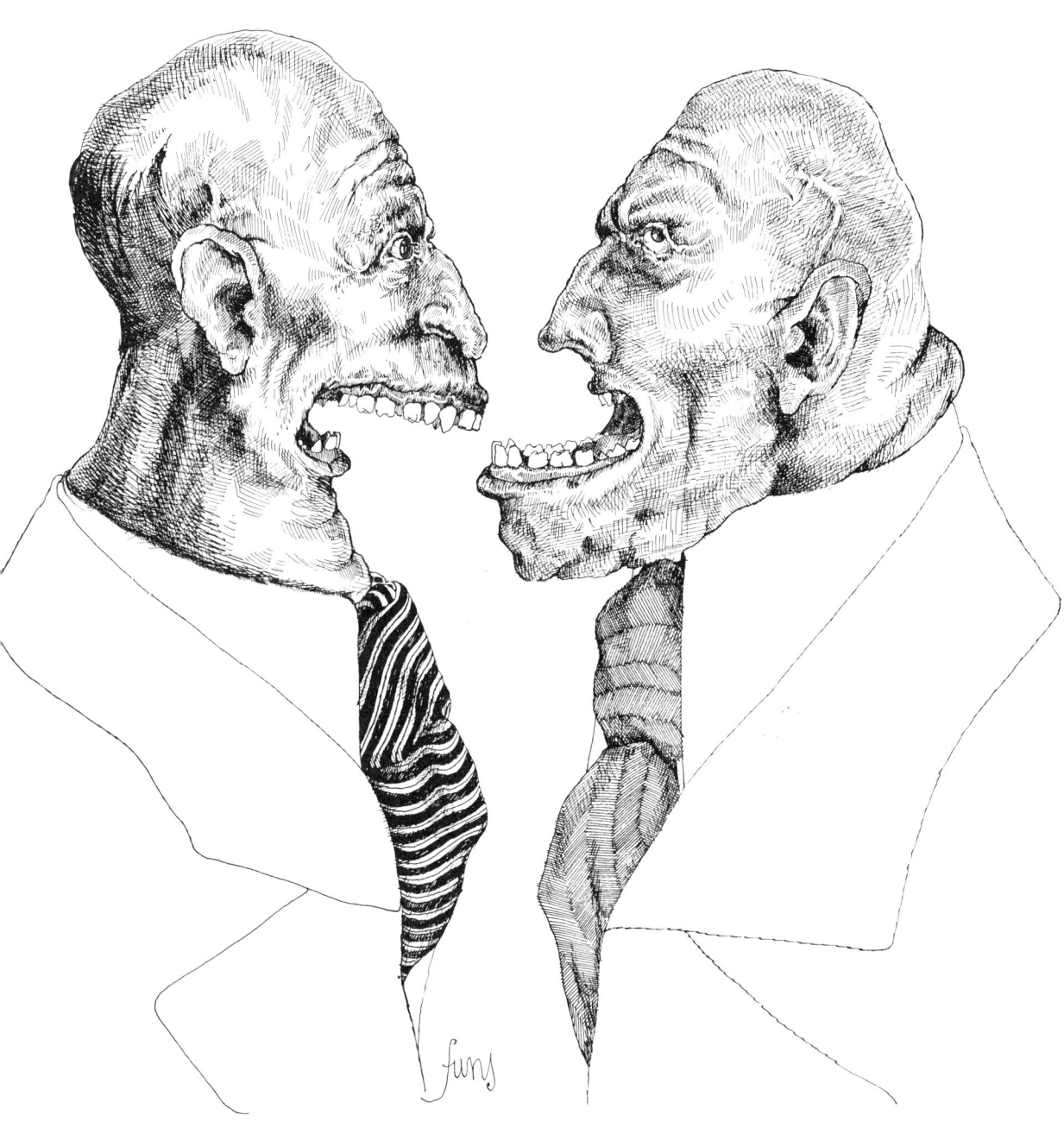

Dedication: To Henriette

THIS IS A BORZOI BOOK PUBLISHED BY ALFRED A. KNOPF, INC.
Copyright © 1970, 1971, 1972, 1973 by Fons van Woerkom
Introduction by Harrison Salisbury Copyright © 1973 by Alfred A. Knopf, Inc.
All rights reserved under International and Pan-American Copyright Conventions.
Published in the United States by Alfred A. Knopf, Inc., New York,
and simultaneously in Canada by Random House of Canada Limited, Toronto.
Distributed by Random House, Inc., New York.
Library of Congress Cataloging in Publication Data
Van Woerkom, Fons.   1. American wit and humor,
Pictorial.   I. Title. NC1429.V36A45   741.5'973
73-7284   ISBN 0-394-70628-5
A number of these drawings first appeared in *The New York Times*,
the Toronto *Daily Star,* and *Penthouse* magazine.
Manufactured in the United States of America
First Edition

INTRODUCTION

When the Op-Ed page of *The New York Times* was conceived in 1970, the question immediately arose of creating a new and total environment embracing words, views, typography, layout, and art. It was hoped that a new dimension could be achieved through a marriage of image and word which would be unlike anything heretofore attempted in print media—something which would enhance the reader's perception, giving resonance to words by images and to images by words.

We recognized that such an ambitious goal would require new forms, new talents, new artists.

Among the first artists brought onto Op-Ed was Fons van Woerkom, whose work we first saw in one of the Canadian papers. We were attracted to him because of his style—which, of course, had little in common with the kind of graphics conventionally used in the American press—and because we felt that his imagination would be capable of creating the environment we sought for the page.

In this expectation we were not disappointed. Fons immediately grasped the challenge of Op-Ed. From the very beginning he contributed some of the most distinguished work we have had the privilege of publishing. His magnificent drawing *Death as Precept*, created for use with the remarkable philosophical observations of Takeshi Muramatsu, constitutes one of the most brilliant combinations of image and word ever achieved by Op-Ed.

Fons' mordant imagery, his deep feeling for the tragic essence of life, for the eternal presence of death in life, is perhaps his strongest philosophical contribution to the atmosphere of Op-Ed.

At times Fons' savage futility becomes almost unbearable, when his mind begins to plumb the depths of man's eternal and desperate confrontation with his own nature and environment. He possesses an extraordinary gift for personal characterization, demonstrated in the conceptions of individuals he has rendered for Op-Ed and other sections of *The New York Times*—General Ridgway, William Buckley, and Harold Macmillan, to select a few classic examples.

It has often puzzled us at Op-Ed that it has been artists of European background who have been most successful in creating the intellectual and emotional milieus essential for our editorial goals. It is my conviction that this is no accident—that artists springing from an alien background of culture bring to America an insight which only a handful of native Americans thus far have been able to demonstrate. Looking at the United States and its world from afar, they penetrate more deeply, reveal more brutally, expose more realistically.

In this genre Fons has demonstrated true mastery.

—HARRISON E. SALISBURY

Guide-lines

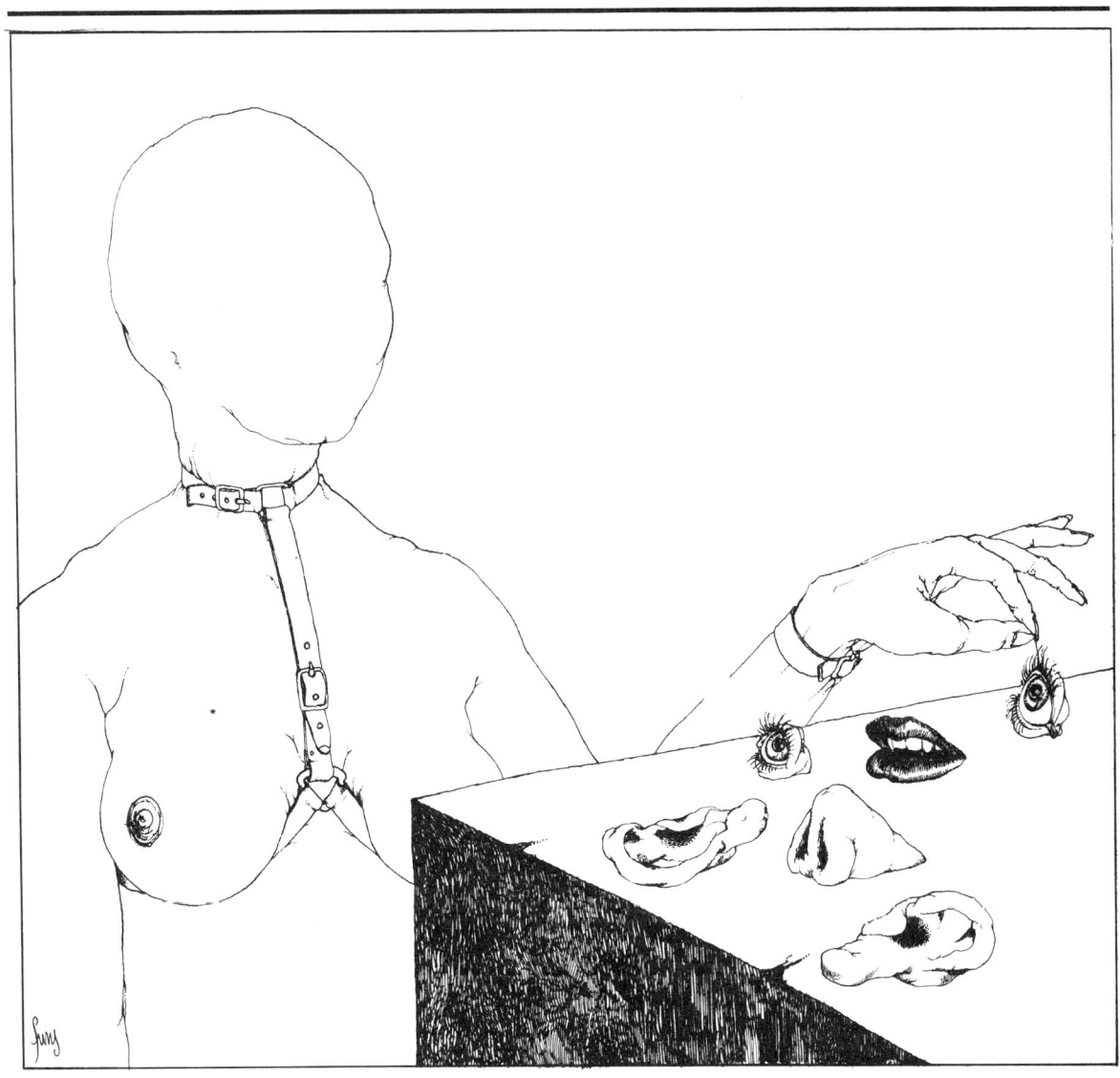

THE DRAWINGS IN "GUIDE-LINES" ARE MAINLY INSPIRED BY MY IMMEDIATE ENVIRONMENT. I HAPPEN TO SEE MANY SELF-DESTRUCTIVE MOTIVATIONS IN THE FACES OF PEOPLE. MAYBE THEY NEED GUIDELINES?   —FONS VAN WOERKOM

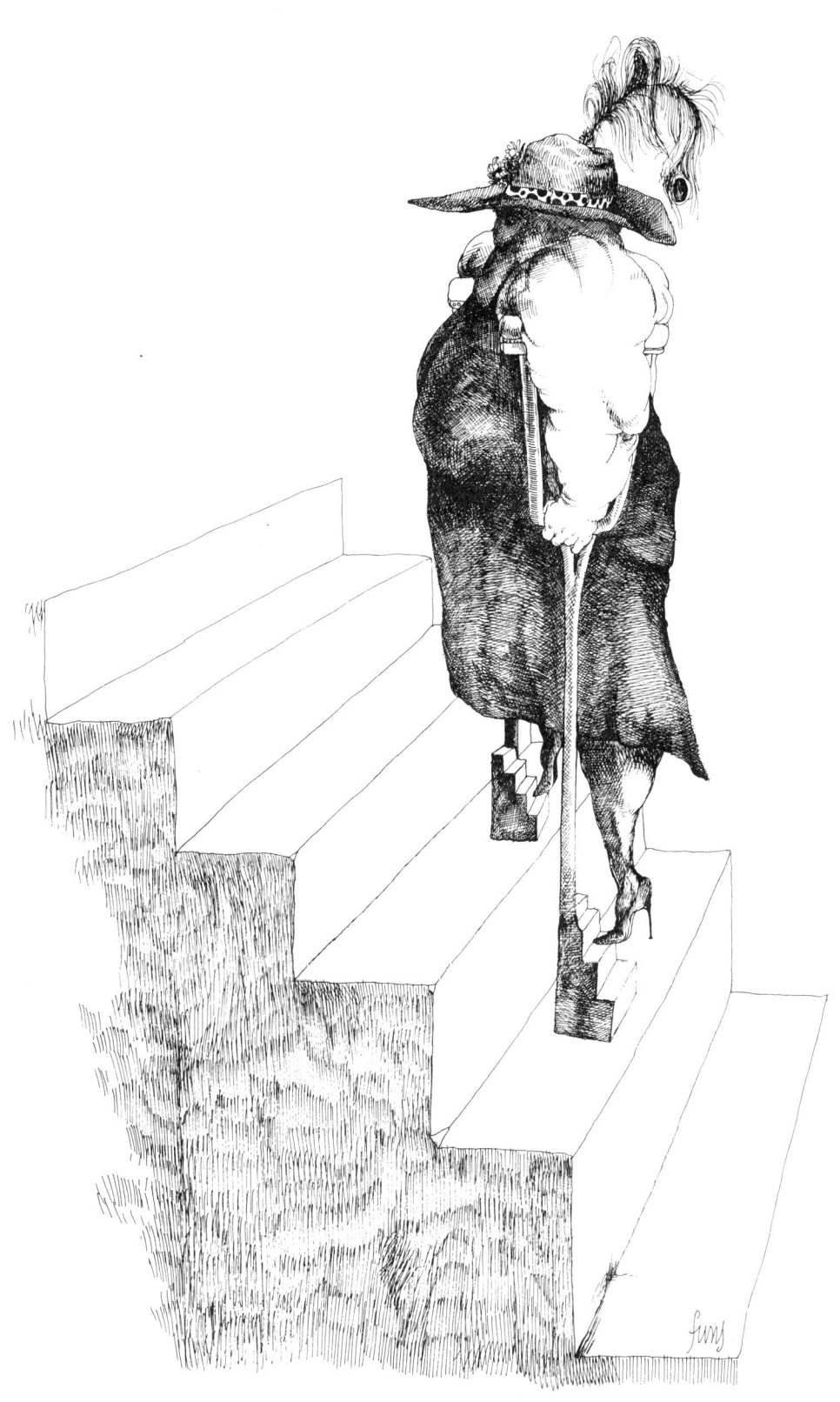

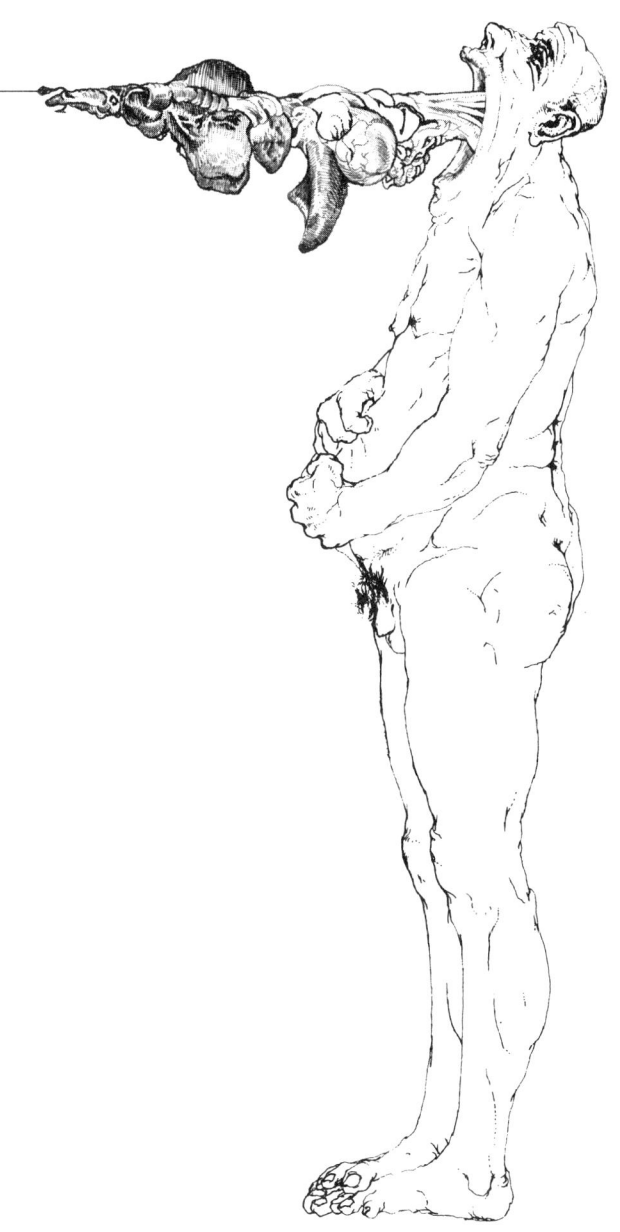

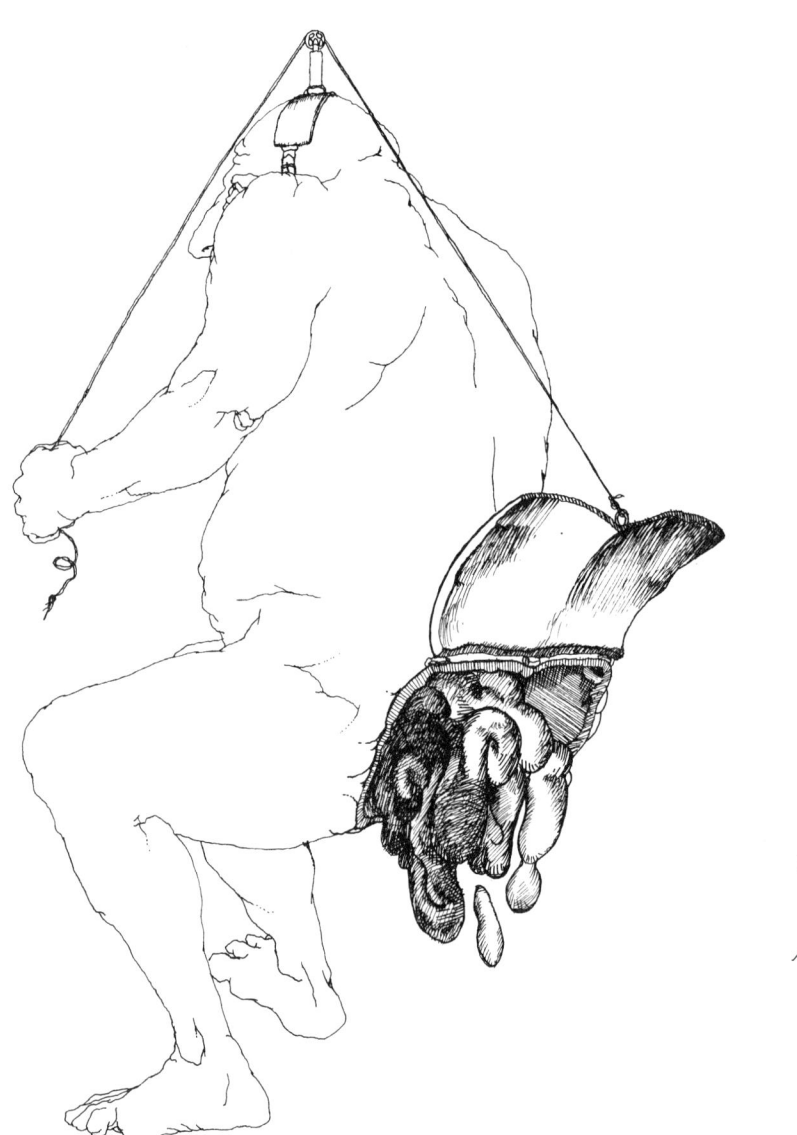

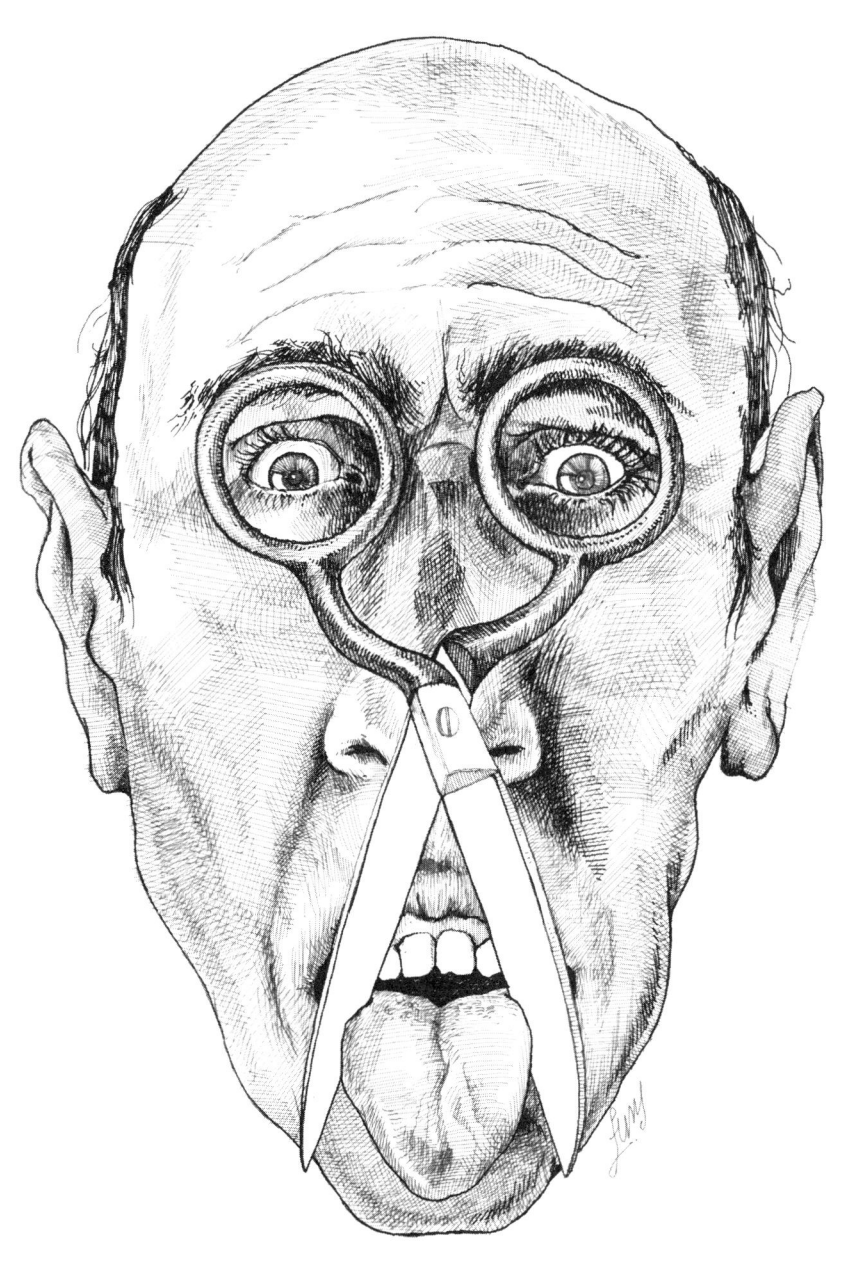

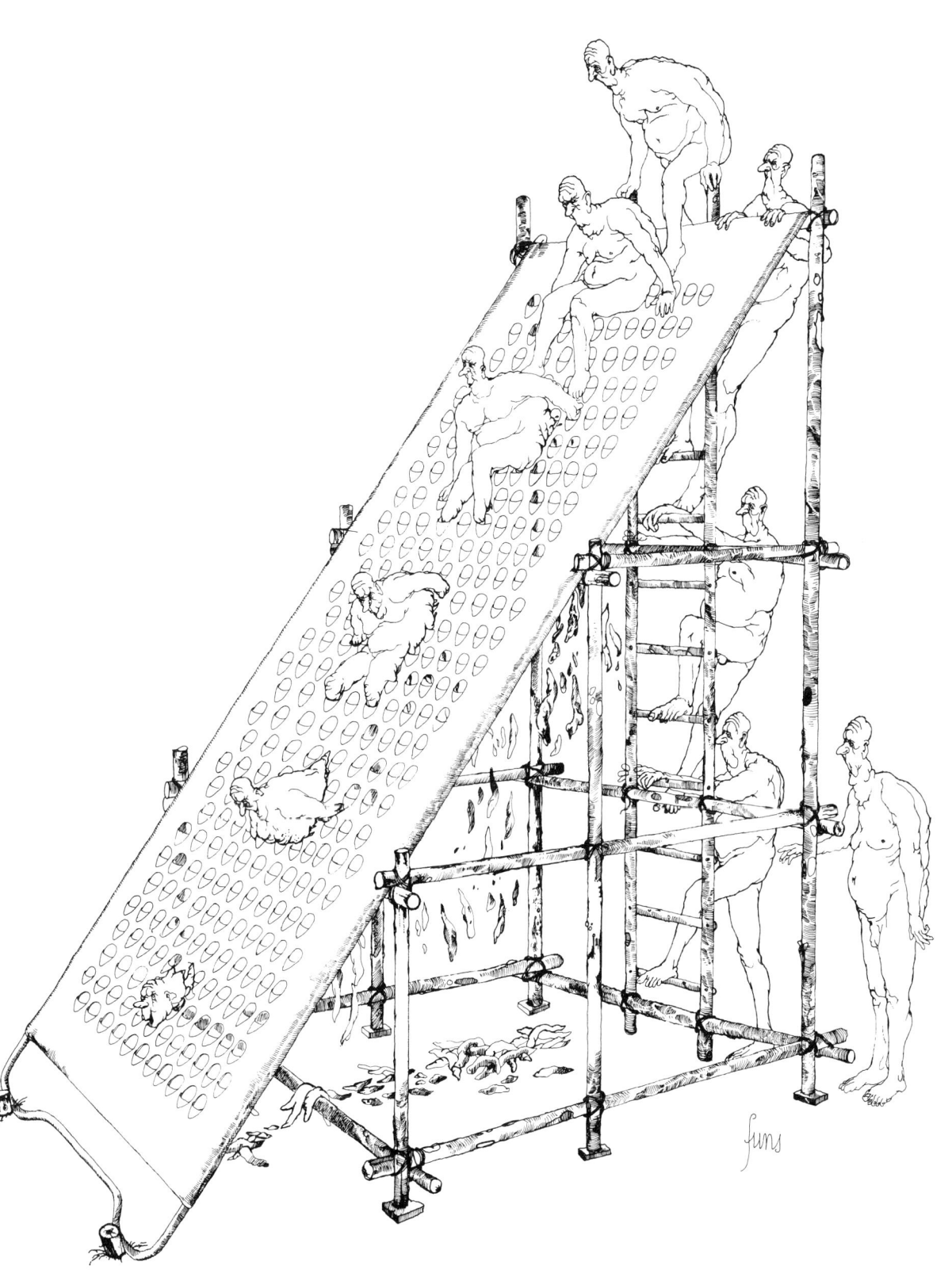

THE CHEESE GRATER

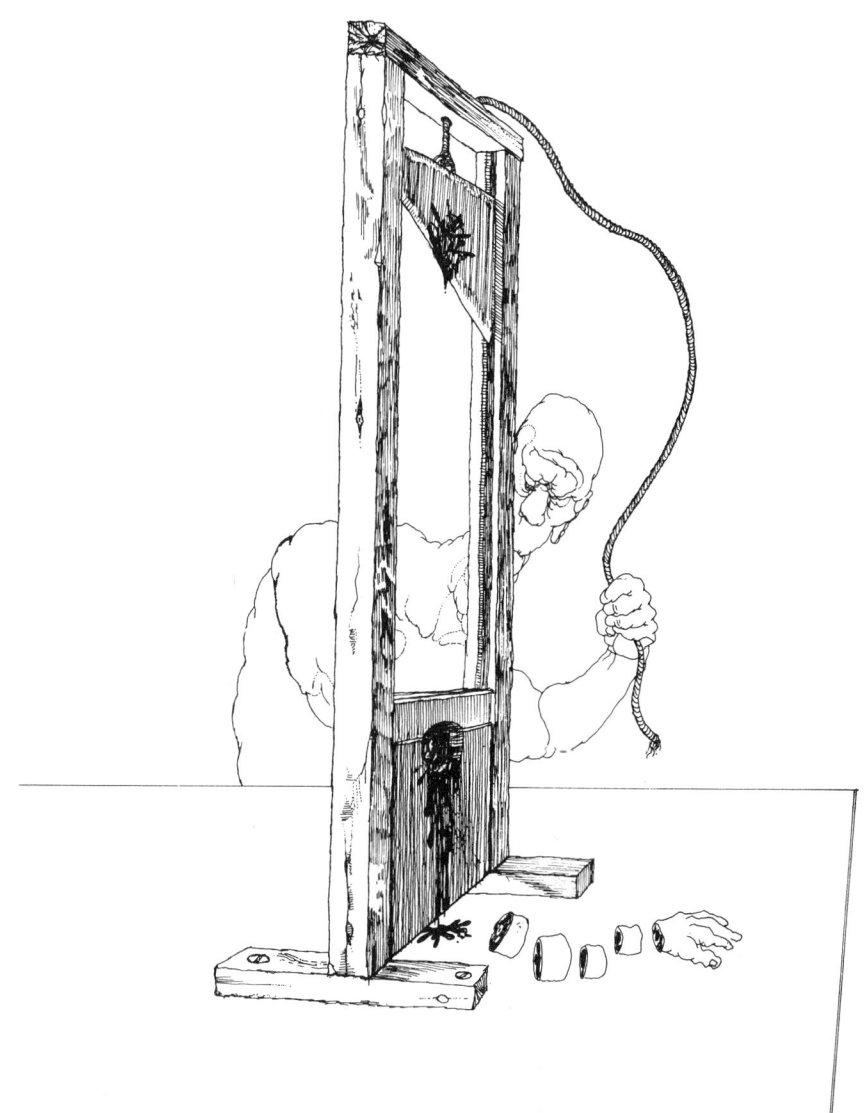

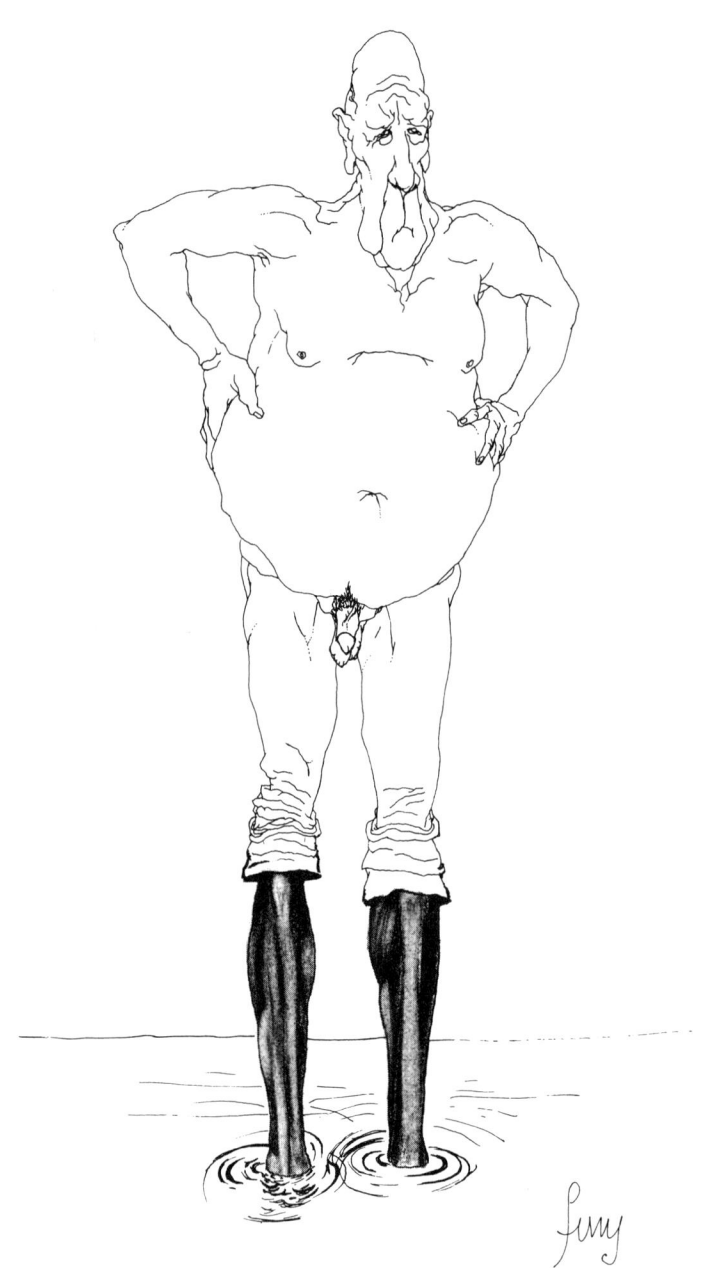

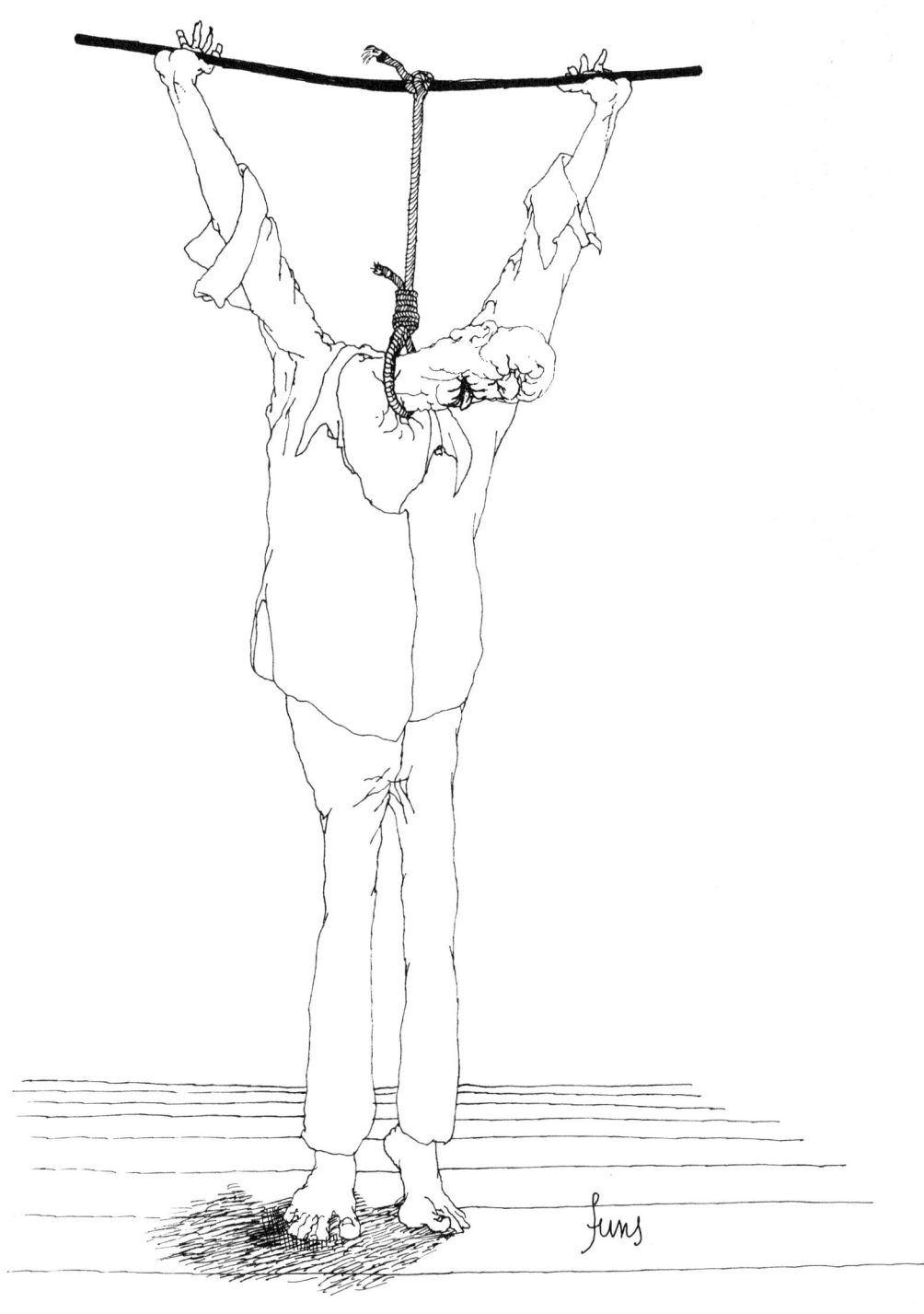

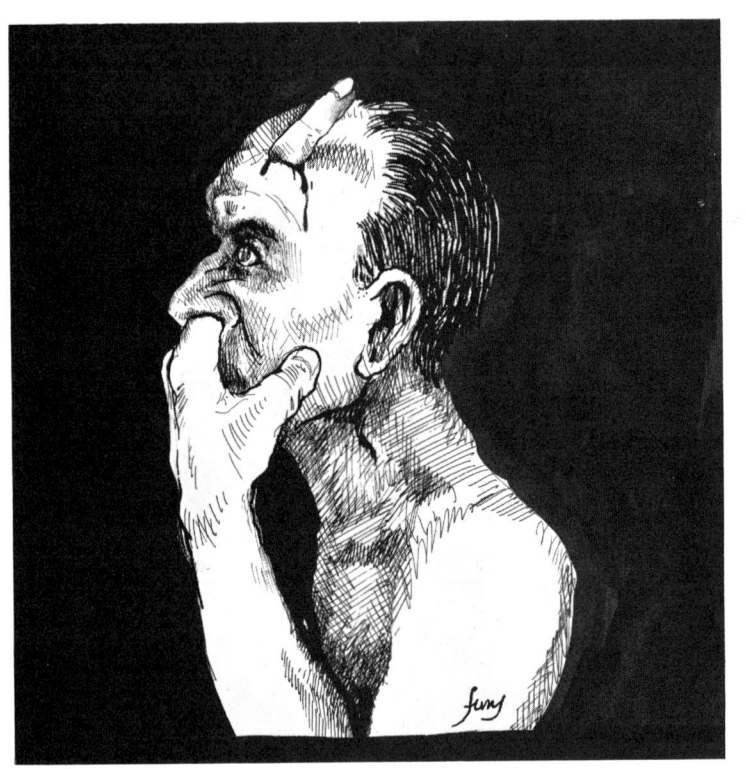

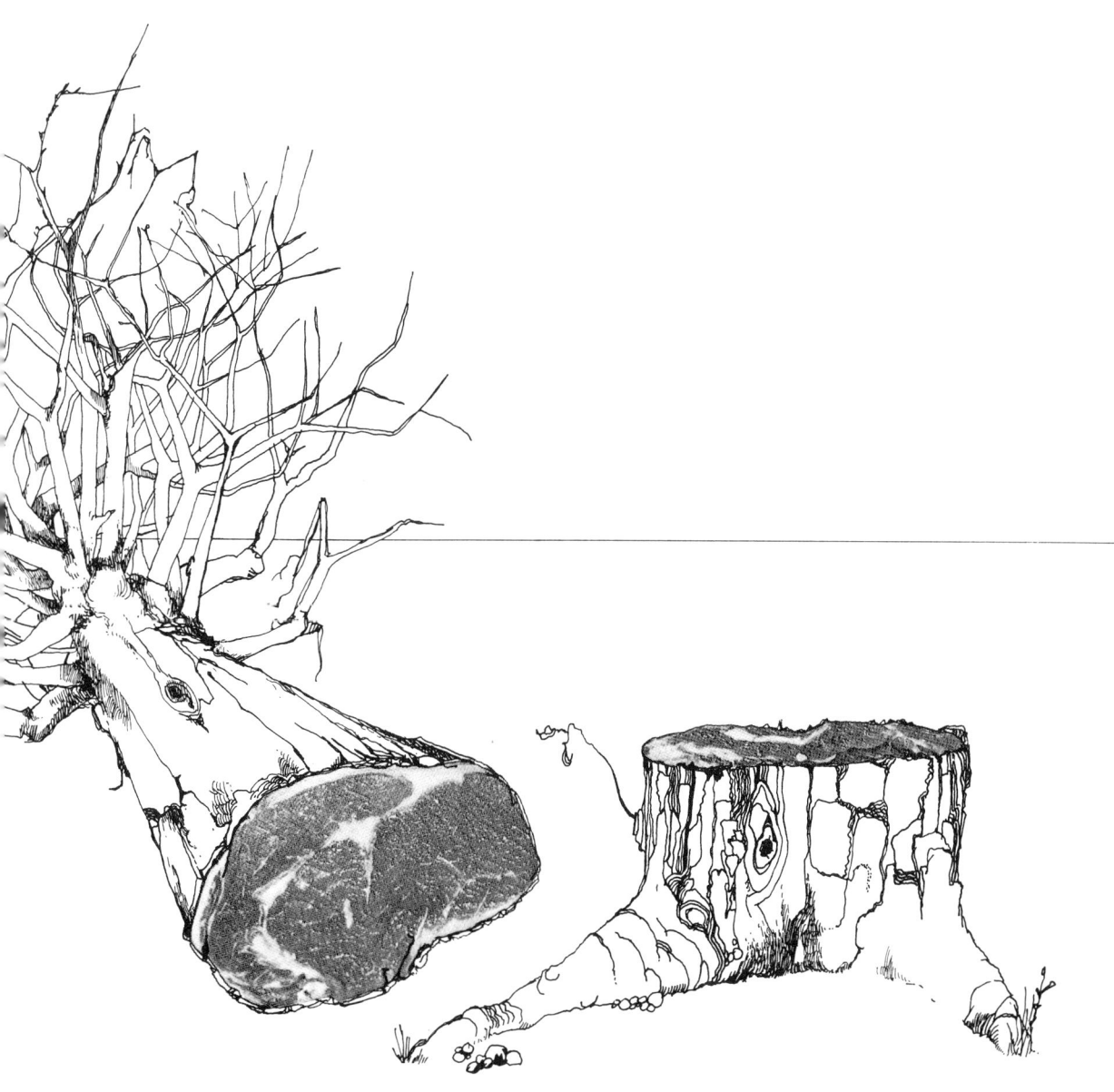

Metamorphosis

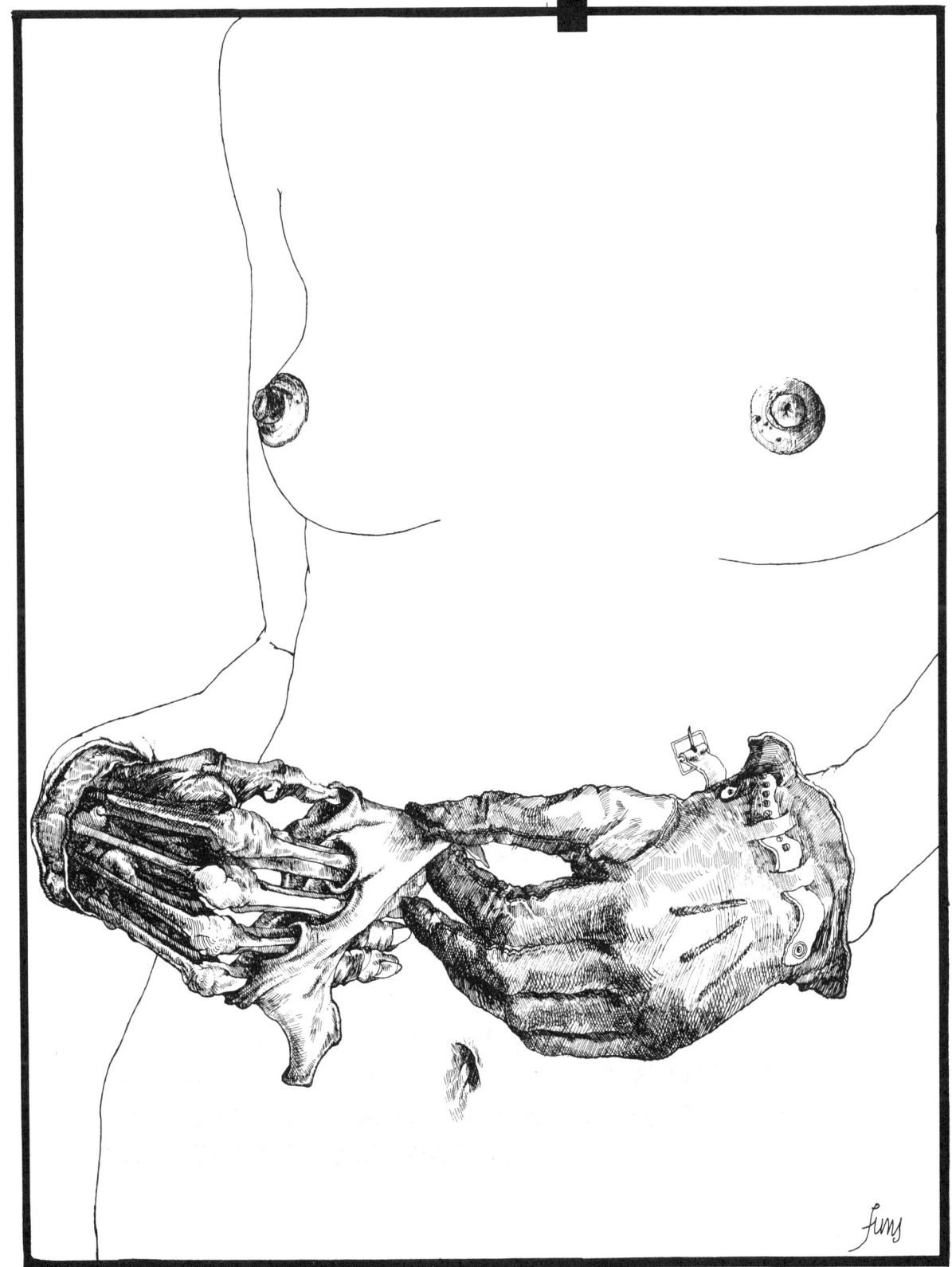

THE DRAWING SEQUENCES OF THE SECOND SECTION ARE ENTIRELY DEVOTED TO WOMEN. A WOMAN FASCINATES ME MORE THAN ANYTHING ELSE. IT SEEMED THAT EVERY TIME I MADE A SINGLE DRAWING THERE WAS A NEED TO EXTEND IT, TO GO ON WITH IT, CREATING A METAMORPHOSIS. THE CLIMAX MARKS THE UNEXPECTED. —FONS VAN WOERKOM

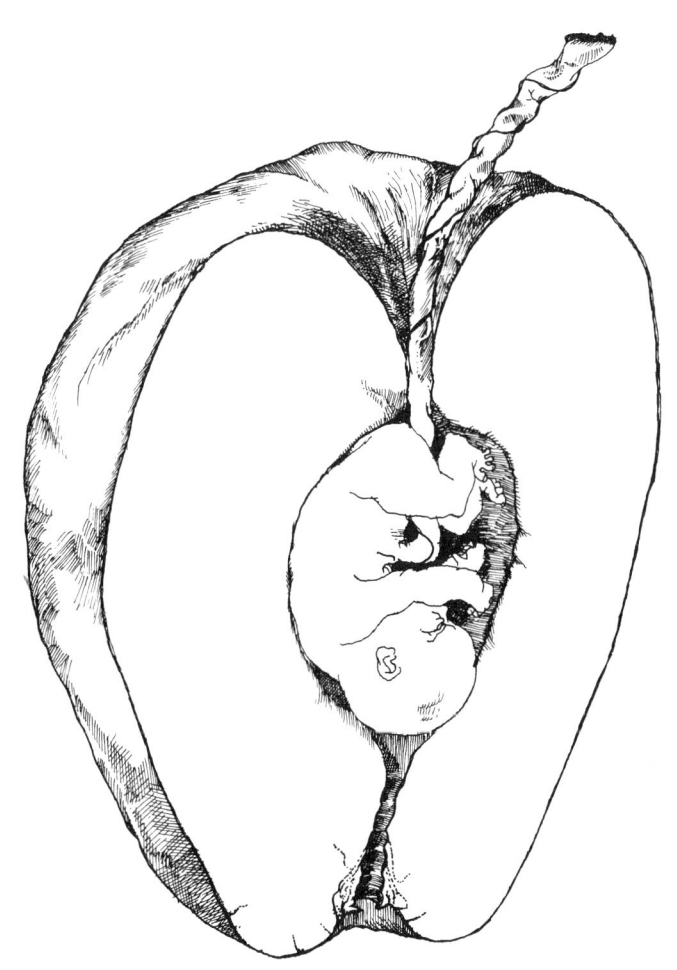

APPLE SEEDLING

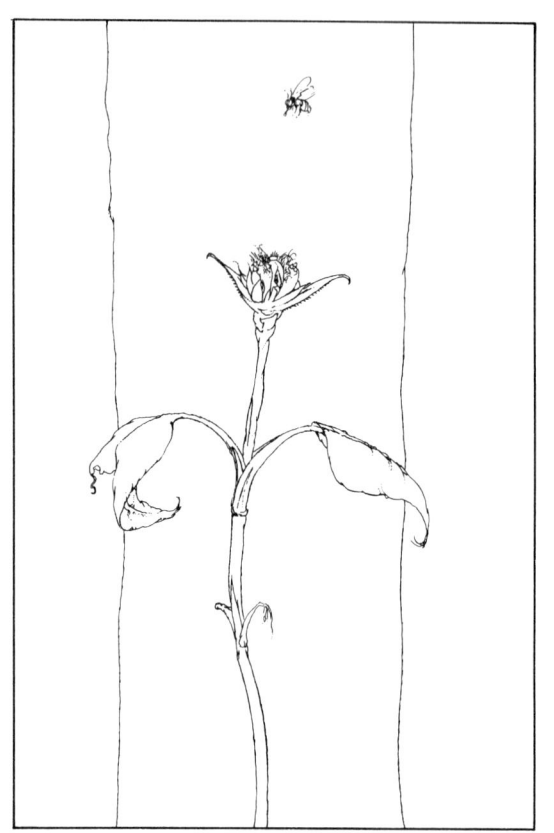 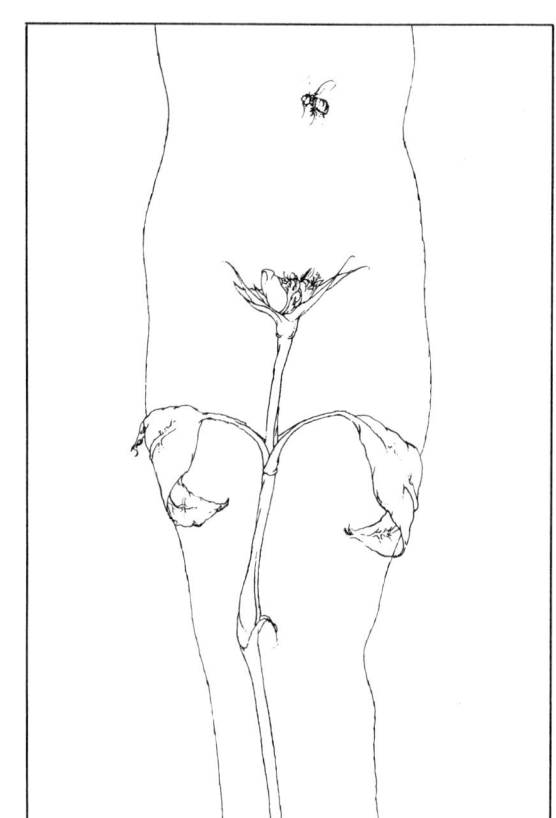

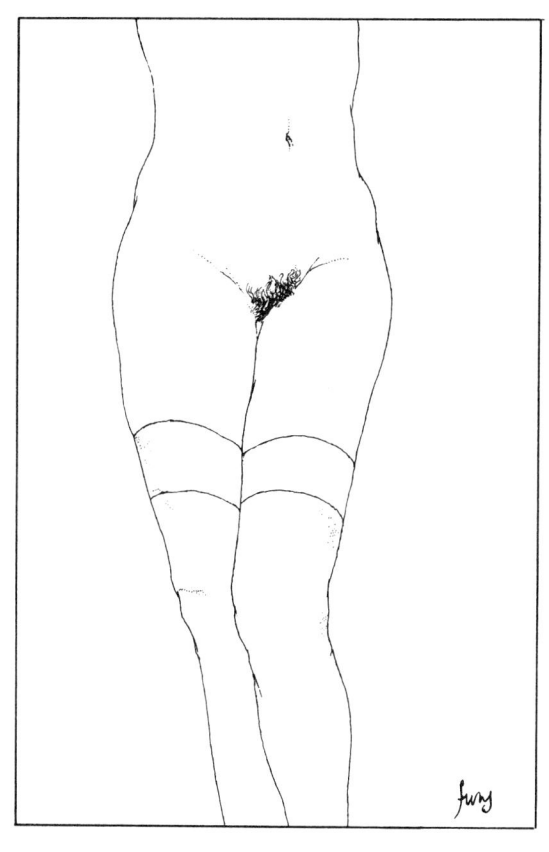
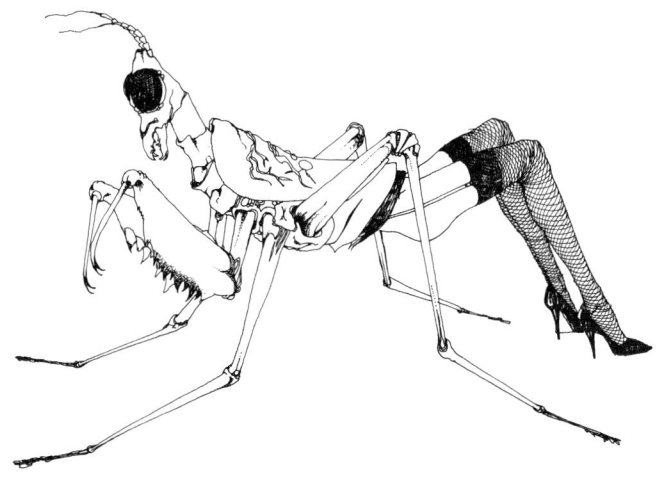

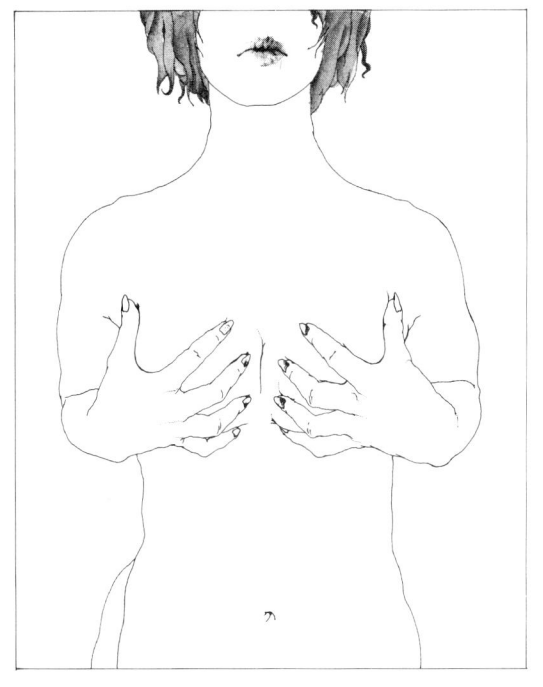
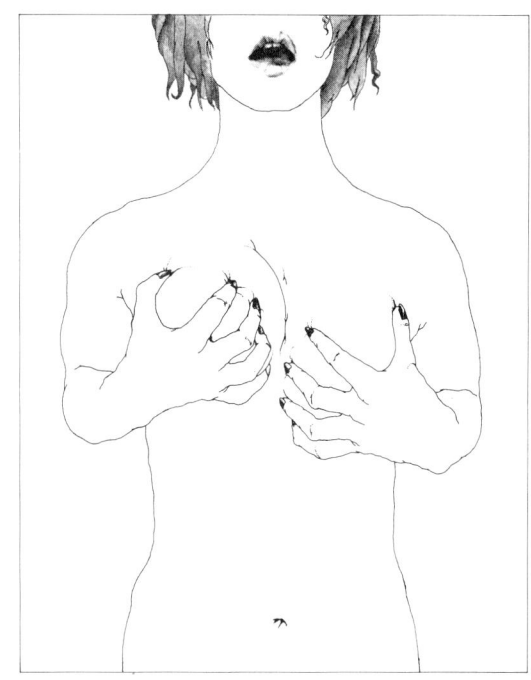
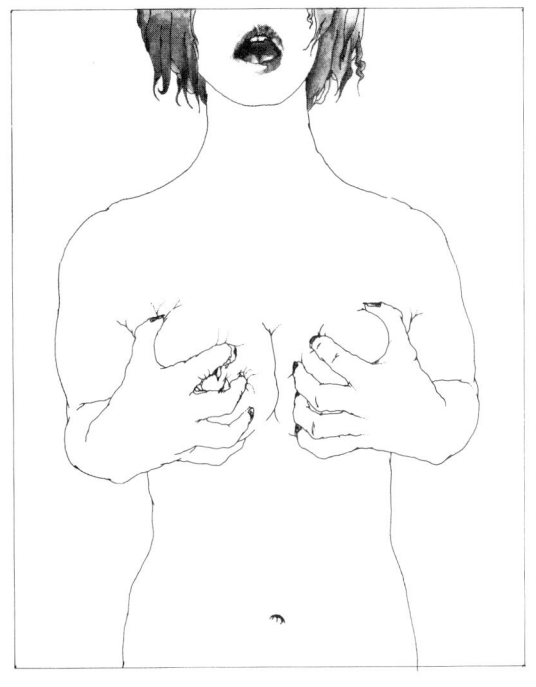
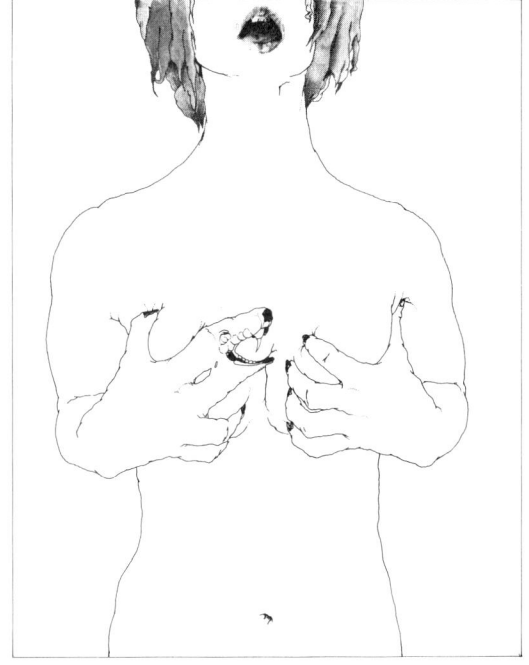

ORGASM

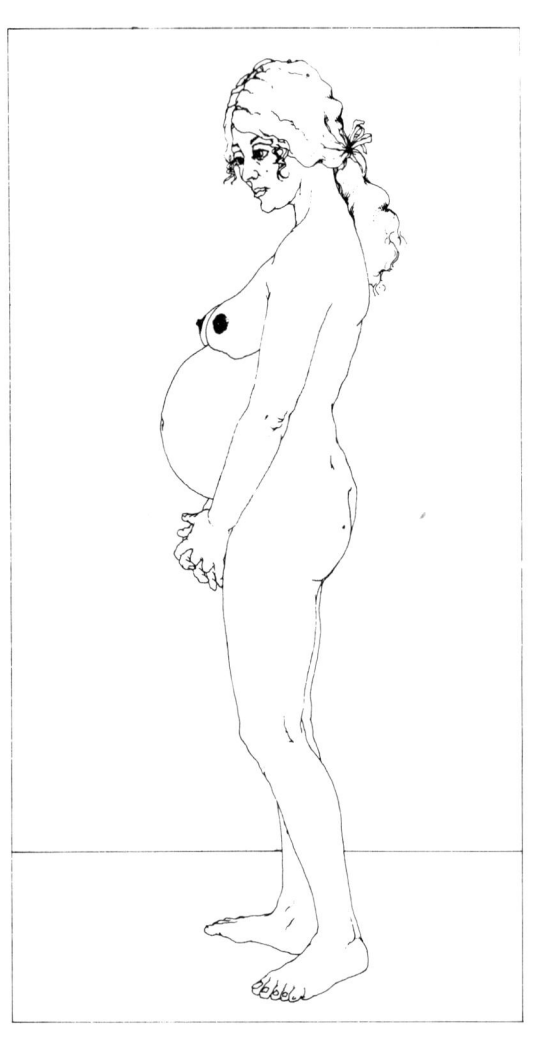 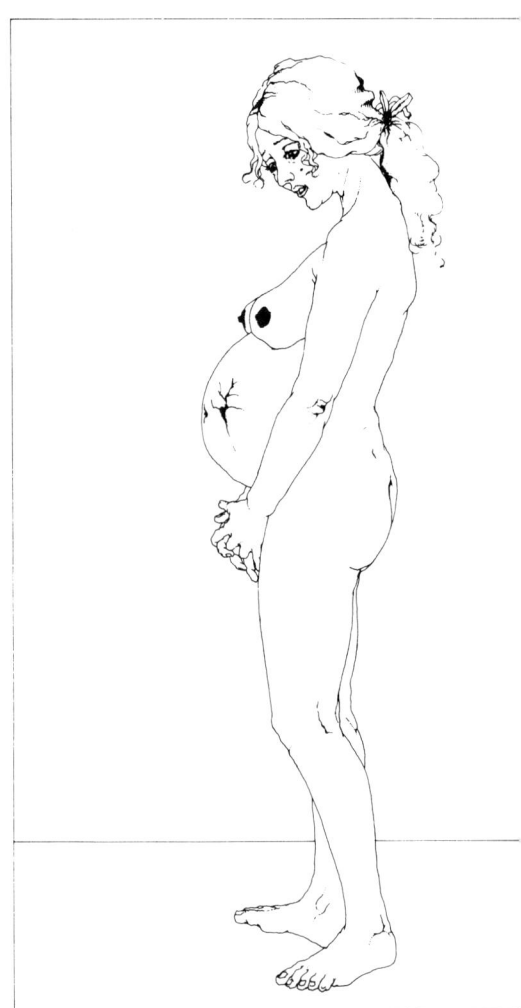

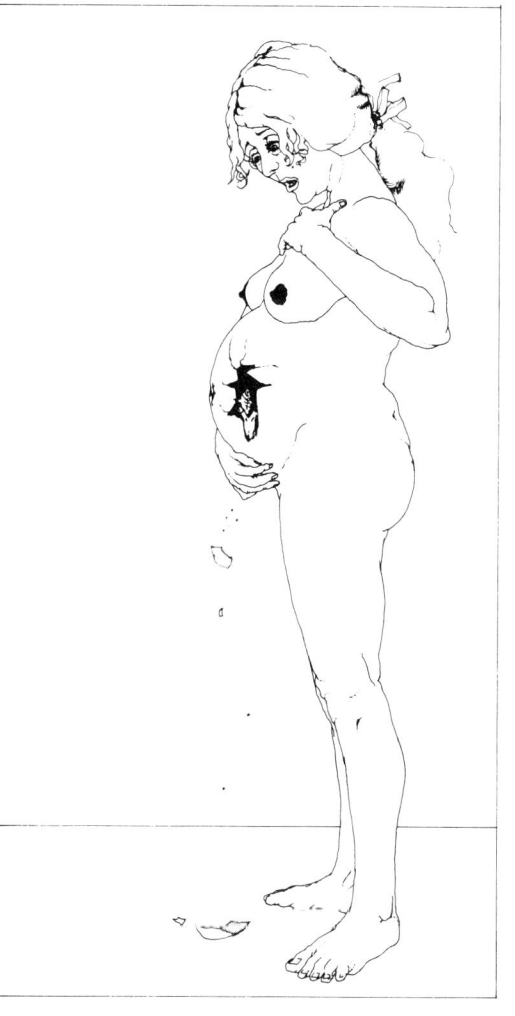

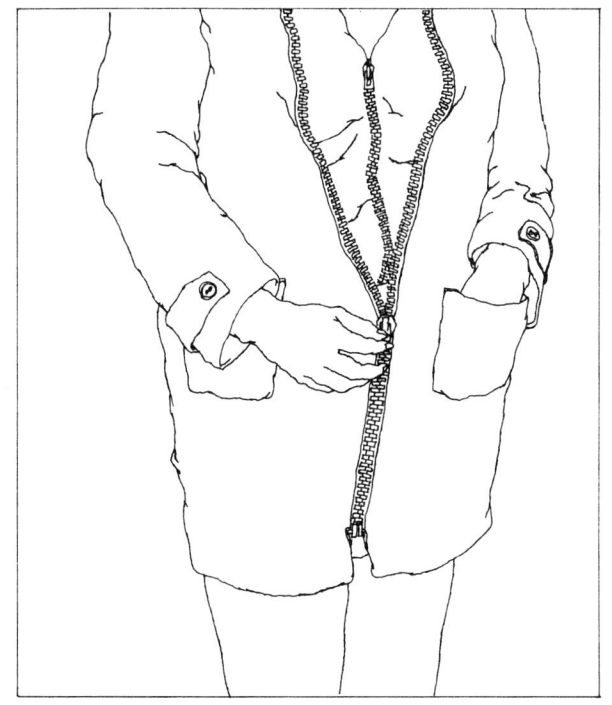

THE ZIPPER

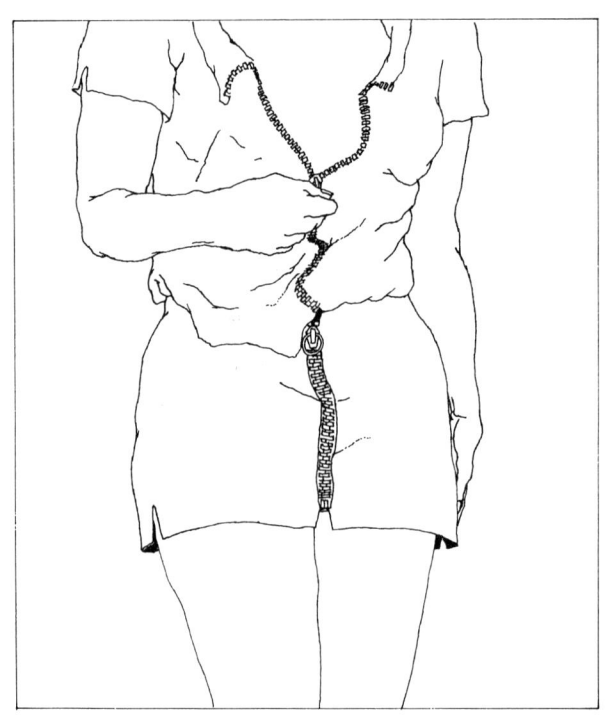

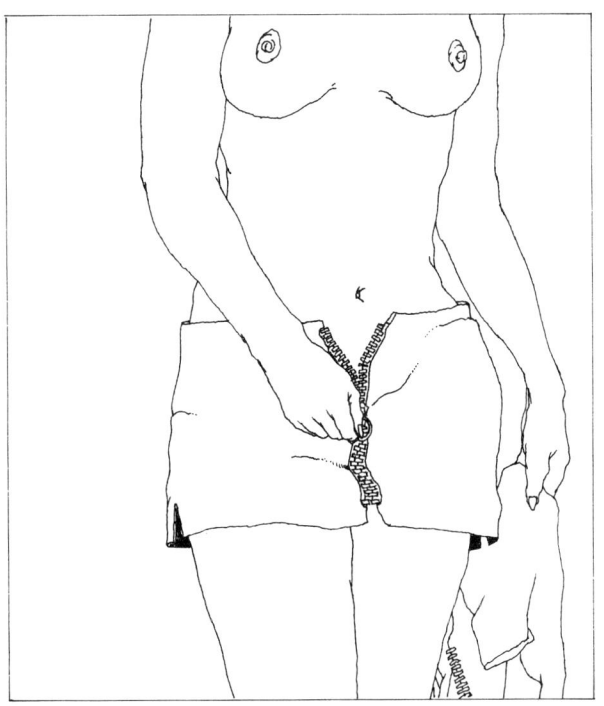

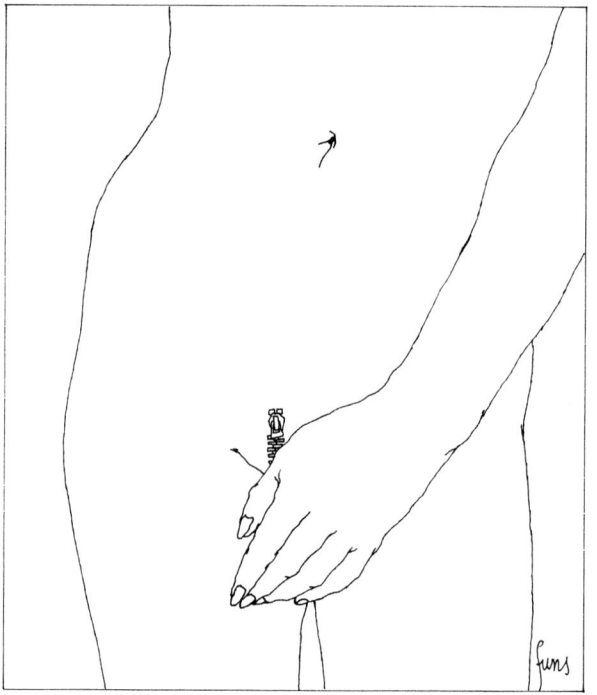

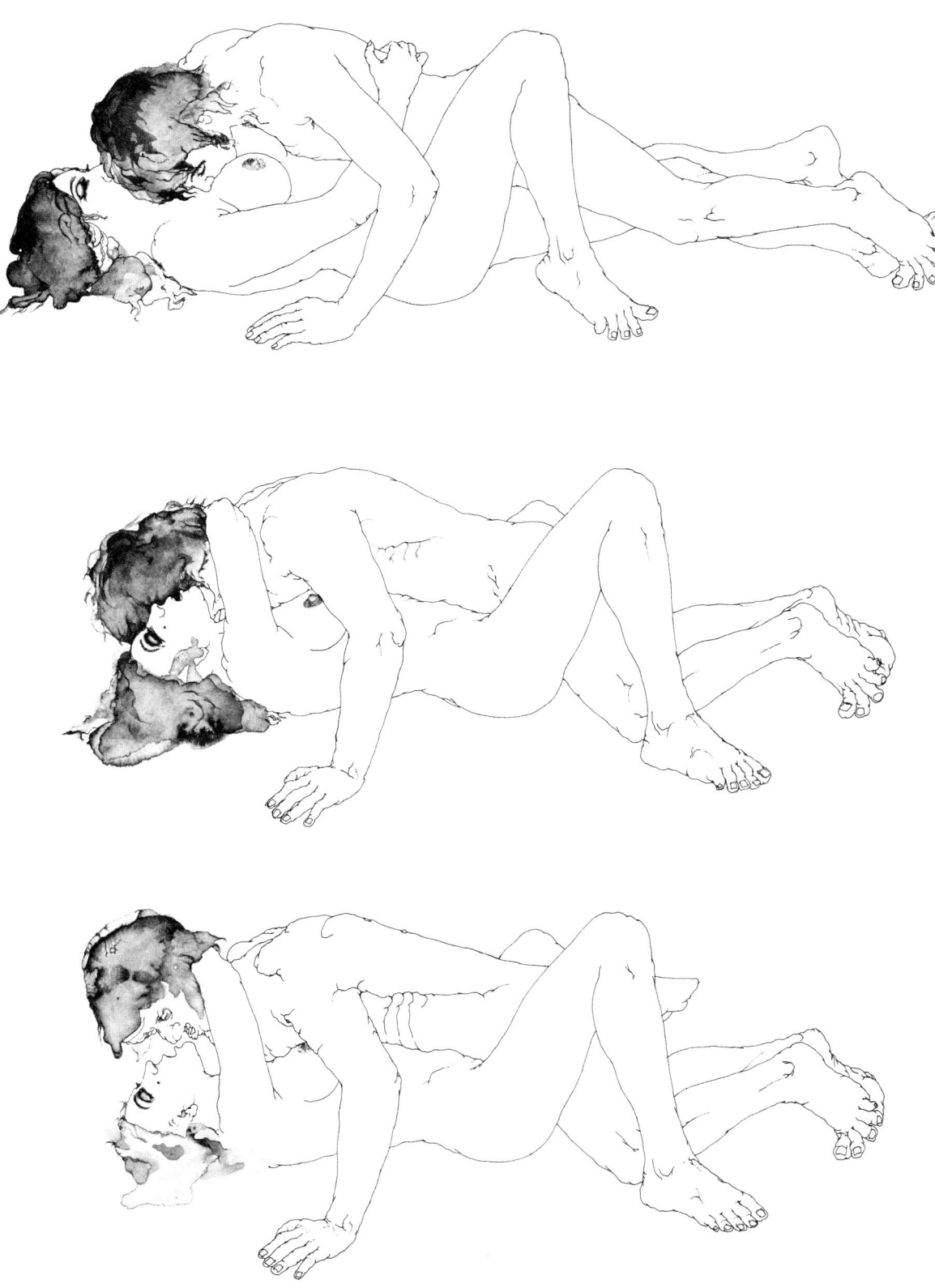

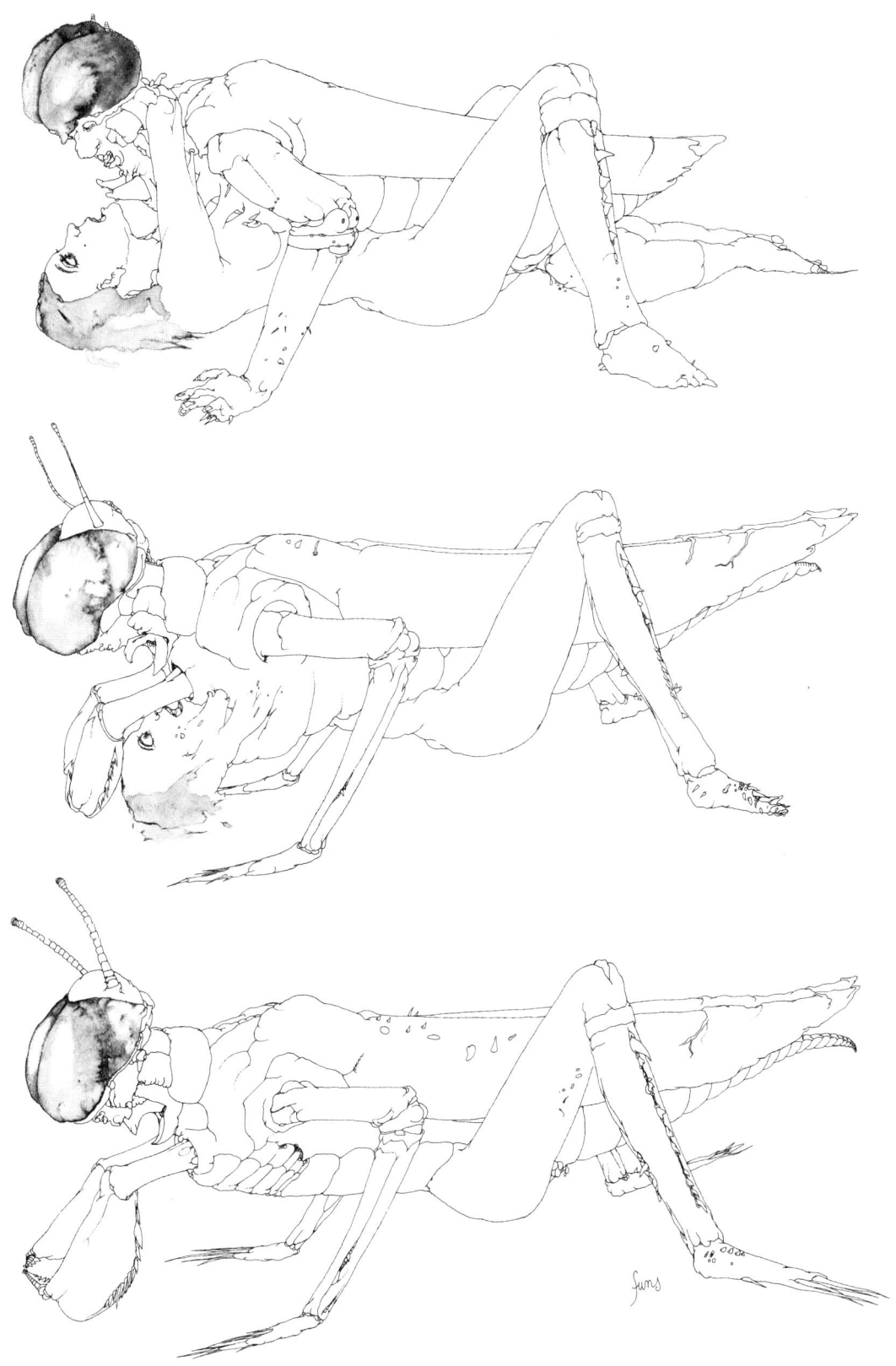

THE GRASSHOPPER

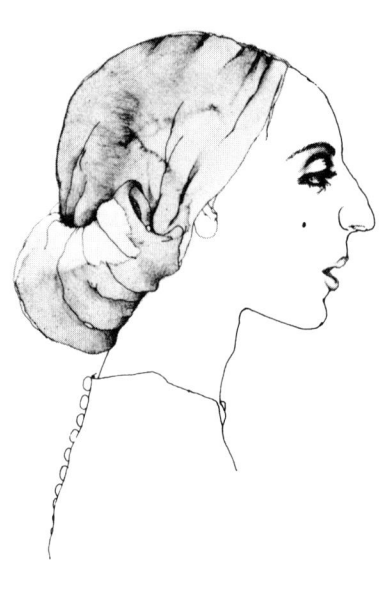
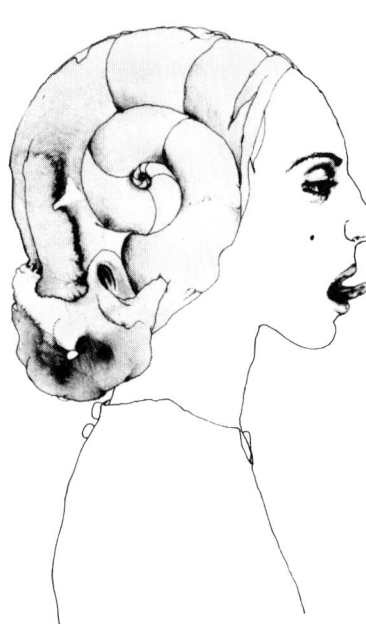

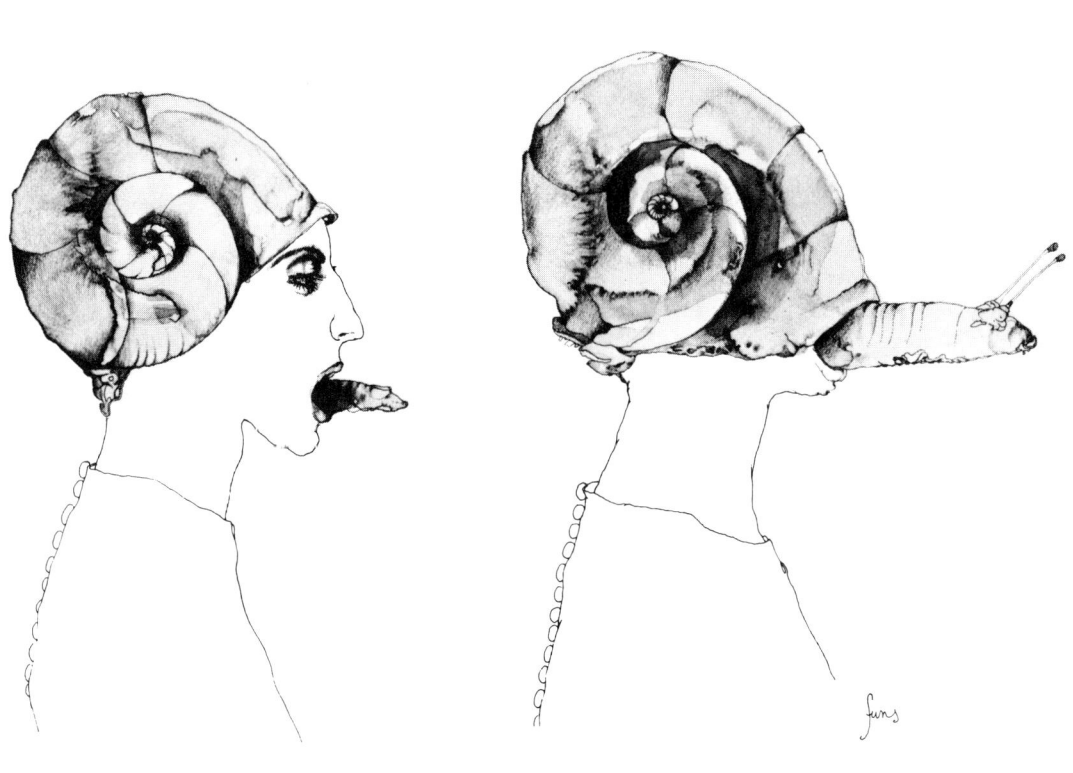

THE SNAIL

METAMORPHOSIS

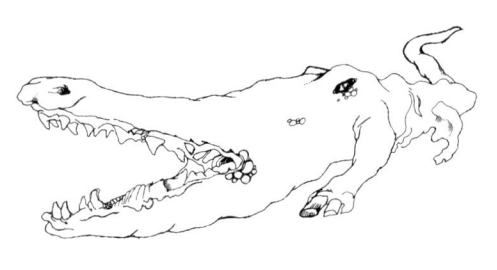

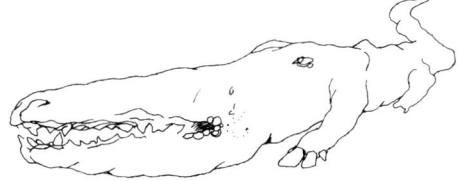

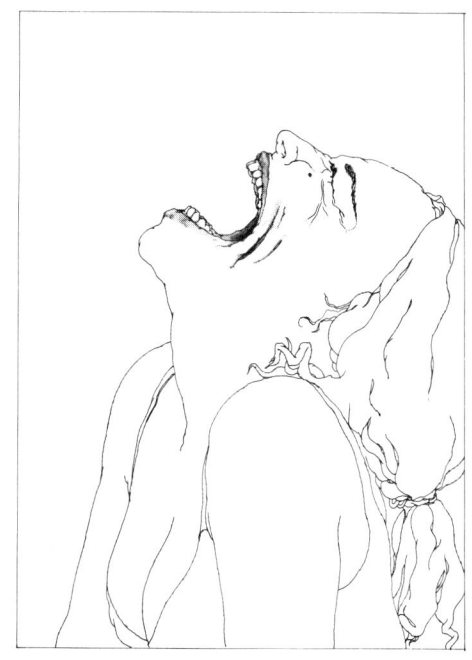

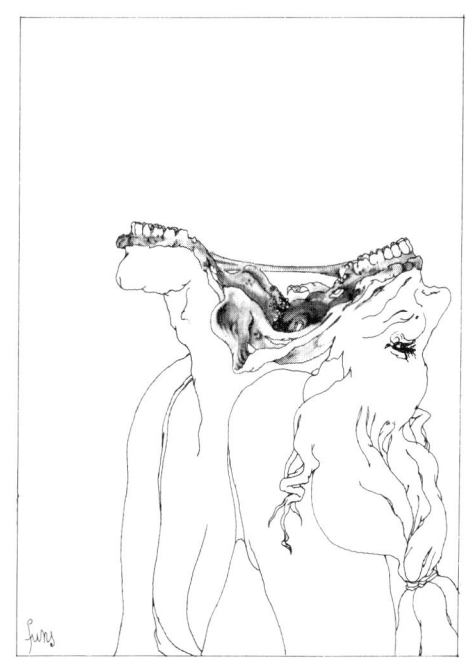

THE LAUGH

THE MOTORCYCLIST

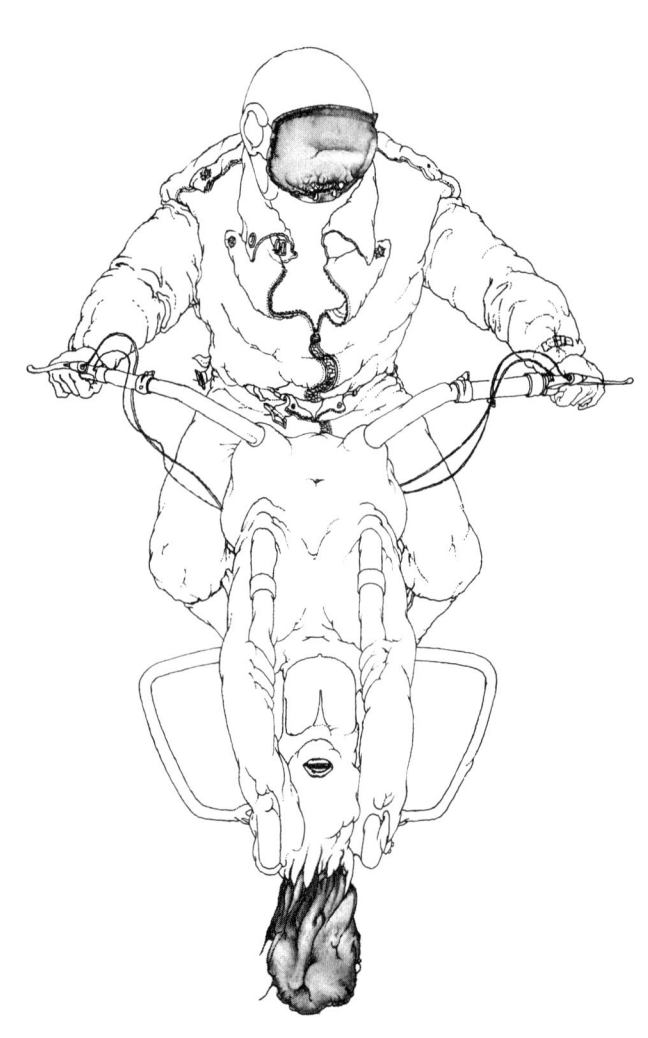

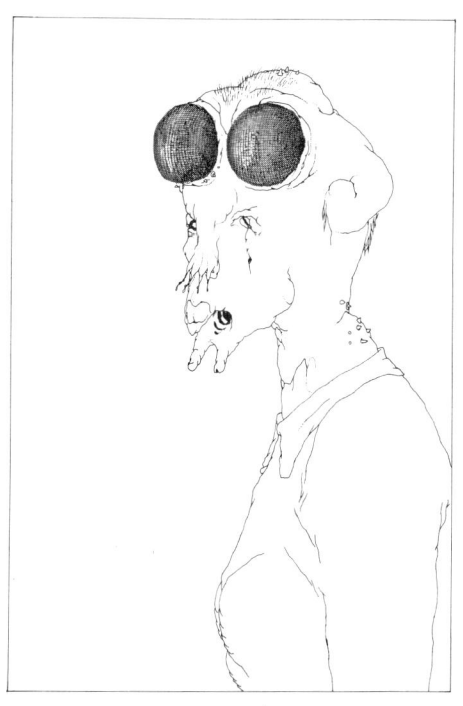
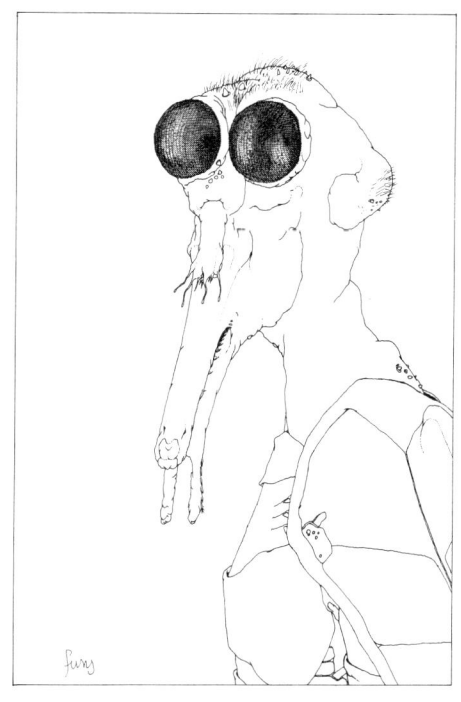

THE SUNGLASSES

THE THOUGHT

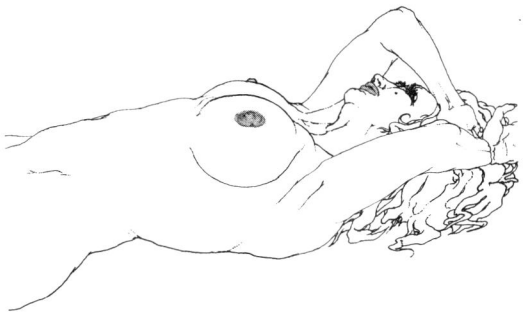

THE STIMULANT

2 P.M. FEEDING

 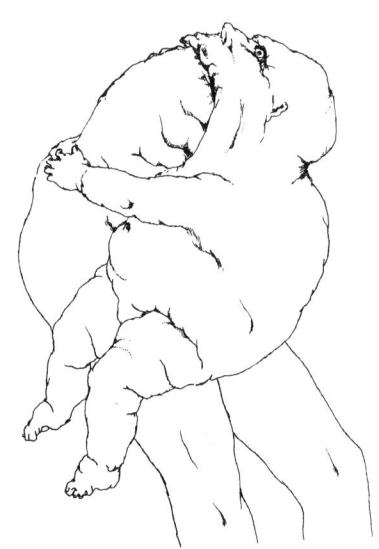

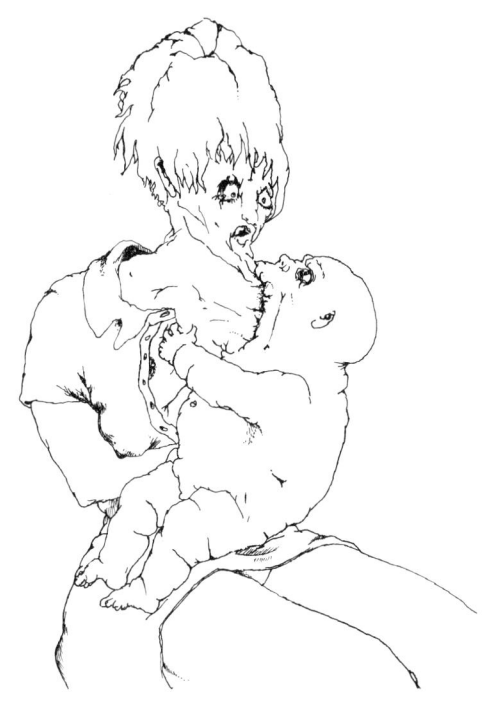
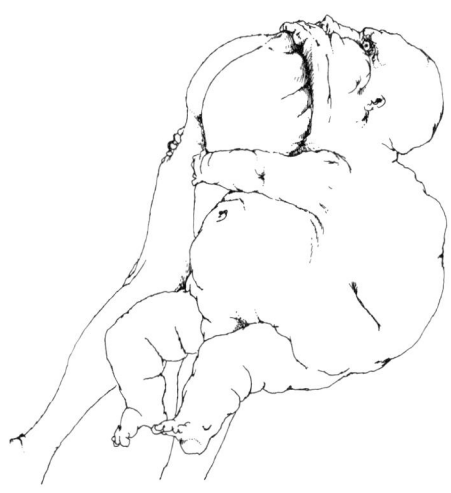

Face to Face

of Vietnam, and that officials in mainland China want to be in on the talks about post-war arrangements.

Also, the talks on nuclear arms control, on a limited Middle East agreement to open the Suez Canal, on the power struggle between East and West Pakistan and on the future of Japan are all reaching an important phase, and the experts believe Peking wants to be sure that it has a voice in shaping events in this vast area, rather than leaving all this to the leadership of the United States and the Soviet Union.

There is general agreement within the Washington Government and the embassies representing governments with missions in Peking that mainland China's sudden change of tone is both hopeful and significant, but officials tend to regard the switch as a tactical move rather than a basic change in Peking's policy.

In fact, the very suddenness of the Chinese move is a warning to the experts not to be too dogmatic about what it means. As President Nixon said in his second annual world report a few weeks ago, a new Asia is emerging; the United States is making substantial cuts in its military forces in Vietnam, Japan, Okinawa, Korea, Thailand and the Philippines; new regional economic arrangements are being made by the nations of the Pacific basin, and in view of all this, it would be surprising if Peking wants to watch these developments in isolation.

But beyond that, the China experts are not willing to predict with any confidence. They agree that Peking would not have started smiling if it really thought Mr. Nixon was going to invade North Vietnam or try to establish permanent military bases in Southeast Asia. They also agree that Peking's move was probably made to minimize Moscow's influence in the post-war settlements rather than to indicate any new spirit of friendliness toward Washington.

So the watchword here is caution. The Sino-Soviet conflict may be irreparable, as most experts seem to believe, but after Mao Tse-tung, nobody is willing to guess about the mood or direction of China. He could be followed by a Khrushchev seeking easier relations with the non-Communist world, or by a Stalin, determined to restore the Moscow-Peking alliance in a more hostile coalition against the West.

Accordingly, modest short-term interpretations are about all the experts are willing to venture. They are

Meanwhile, President Nixon is being given credit here for making it easy for Peking to take a more cooperative attitude. Despite his long record of hostility toward Peking before he came into the White House, he has recently been offering them an honorable compromise and recognizing their place as one of the great nations in the world.

"In this decade," he said in his last world report, "there will be no more important challenge than that of drawing the People's Republic of China into a constructive relationship with the world community.... We see no advantage to us in the hostility between the Soviet Union and Communist China. We do not seek any. We will do nothing to sharpen that conflict—nor to encourage it.

"We are prepared to establish a dialogue with Peking. We cannot accept its ideological precepts or the notion that Communist China must exercise hegemony over Asia.... Our attitude is public and clear. We will continue to honor our commitments [to Nationalist China] and to the security of our Asian allies (including Nationalist China). An honorable relationship with Peking cannot be constructed at their expense."

Thus the problem of the "two Chinas" remains, as it has for many years. Twenty-one years ago it seemed that there was another chance to compose the differences between Washington and Peking and bring Communist China into the United Nations, but the chance was lost.

"I have now come to believe," said John Foster Dulles in 1950, "that the United States will best serve the cause of peace if its Assembly is representative of what the world actually is, and not merely representative of the parts which we like....

"If the Communist Government of China in fact proves its ability to govern China without serious domestic resistance, then it too should be admitted to the United Nations.... Communist governments today dominate more than 30 per cent of the population of the world. We may not like that fact. Indeed, we do not like it at all. But if we want to have a *world* organization, then it should be representative of the world as it is."

That was a whole generation ago, and Communist China is still outside the U.N., but it has a real chance this year to get the votes for membership, and this may be one more reason why Peking is changing its tune.

Uncle Sam Looks South

By C. L. SULZBERGER

FOREIGN AFFAIRS

JOHANNESBURG, South Africa—Any South American tour forces certain conclusions that are best reported immediately, even from another continent. The first conclusion is that there has been a major change in relations with North America. The Monroe Doctrine's inherent philosophy that developed into an effort to exclude foreign powers from a market where the U.S.A. sought outlets for its capital surplus is now wholly outdated. One wry joke heard in Latin lands is: "The Alliance for Progress must be succeeding; we are getting a better class of dictator."

Juscelino Kubitschek, former Brazilian President, says: "Kennedy made a profound psychological error in creating the Alliance. He should have consulted Latin nations but, in effect, he told them: 'I will do this.' Johnson forgot Latin America—except the Dominican Republic. Nixon won't even hear of it. No popular feeling exists here that the U.S. really wants to help this continent."

Kubitschek proposes that the U.S.A. give no money to Latin countries but should help finance national development plans through necessary technical assistance.

This, in fact, is already Nixon's policy as expressed in last month's State Department report which suggested "more effective development assistance, set increasingly in a multilateral framework."

Ten years ago when I talked with West European ambassadors on another Latin-American tour they said: "Whenever we mention increasing our investment we hear the word 'Monroe Doctrine.'" Today the situation is reversed. Washington realizes rising nationalism is "directed against foreign investment, particularly our own." One way to reduce the onus is to share the burden.

The wisest course would be for Washington, which insures them, to urge U.S. companies to try whenever possible to enter into joint South American enterprises with such friend-

copper crisis and even in Brazil trouble will come if the above rule is ignored.

We have learned two other lessons: that the United States cannot rely on Latin America as a market for its military equipment or as a mirror for its ideology. The southern countries have turned increasingly to other weapons sources because we kept offering inadequate matériel. Now the size of our military missions steadily shrinks.

Our dominance is far from absolute in our own backyard and even the possibility of intervention has almost if not entirely vanished. We can only influence events and often but minor events. Moreover, few ideological regimes south of the Rio Grande are of the sort we fully admire. The Latin nature doesn't easily lend itself to Anglo-Saxon political prejudices.

True democrats like Kubitschek or Frei in Chile are disappointed with our philosophical posture. Kubitschek says: "The U.S. should really lead the democratic world, supporting all who fight for democratic institutions. It should give ideological and moral leadership not material leadership. A successful campaign for democracy cuts into both right and left and could help Latin America break out of the extremist alternatives, which otherwise may fall eventually on the side of Communism."

Traditional U.S. efforts to control South American mineral wealth and dominate industry cannot swiftly be erased and the tendency of many U.S. communities to live in self-chosen ghettos of comfort amid their Latin fellows has heightened the jealousy felt by poor for rich. Moreover, counter-terrorist campaigns conducted by rightist governments rub off on the U.S.A., which is seen as condoning reaction for the sake of stabilizing its investment security.

The first step, in the interests of everyone concerned, is to energize the

NewArk at all, but who simply come to work or do business here, then go home to their version of paradise.

The fact of NewArk as a huge violent slum ignited, all but destroyed, and reignited by the racism and disregard of a well-fed, exploiting absentee landlord white supracommunity in the suburbs should be well known by now. It led to the explosion of August 1967.

When we spoke of political self-determination and a black mayor in those days it was dismissed by many as racism. To want to have black people govern a city in which they were the clear overwhelming majority was termed (by racists) racism. But it was the evolution of blacks and Puerto Ricans from out of our "minority mentality" to grasp the fact that we were the majority here, which brought about the election of Mayor Kenneth Gibson last June, and the beginnings of representative government and political equity (still not complete). It was also part of the continuing movement by that majority community, in the spirit of "operational unity," to achieve real political, economic and institutional self-determination, self-respect and self-defense.

The achievement of these goals is

manifestation of this same power addiction and lack of understanding. (And I say teachers' union strike since the majority of teachers are teaching and just about all the schools are open, and have been since the beginning of the strike.) The union feels it must have control over the educational process in NewArk. But the union is largely white and suburban, the neighbors of the absentee landlords. The union's salary demands are completely out of line with the community's economic level and life style. They want 10,000 dollars a year and a welfare fund in a city where there is over 25 per cent unemployment in the black community.

The union says that its members should not have to perform so called "nonprofessional" chores, such as bringing children from classroom to cafeteria, or from schoolbus to classroom, or collect bank money. If the union does not even want that human a relationship with the children, why should it want to teach them in the first place the community asks. But the community is not out to "break the union." We are out to protect our children and raise the quality of edu-

want the power to control the "space" we are in, not just geographic, but institutional, political and economic.

The constant attempts to show Mayor Gibson as the captive of "ultra militants" is bizarre. The nationalist community of NewArk is a legitimate part of Mayor Gibson's constituency.

Mayor Gibson could not effectively govern NewArk without hearing all sides of all questions, including the black nationalist side, whom we, at the Committee for a Unified NewArk, represent. We are neither "ultramilitants" (as The Times has described us apparently in an attempt to see that we fit the bullseye of somebody's genocidal target, as a replacement for the Panthers) nor "bodyguards," but instead young Africans being educated to the realities of American life, who are, at the same time, the undiminishable core of black concern, whose role is, as we see it, to restore our people to their traditional greatness.

Imamu Amiri Baraka, also known as LeRoi Jones, is a poet, playwright and head of the Committee for a Unified NewArk, which has adopted the distinctive spelling for the city where it is based.

in a diplomatic service, no government can afford to keep its public fully informed on what it does in the field of international relations. Sometimes it must conceal the reasons for its actions, and sometimes the actions themselves. In some rare instances, it must pretend to be taking one set of actions while actually taking another, and to present the public with a largely fictional picture of what it is doing and why.

This is especially true when our State Department comes up against a problem such as the Arab-Israel conflict. A diplomat newly assigned to this particular problem finds himself in the possession of "estimates of the situation" provided by the C.I.A., the Pentagon, and embassies reporting from Israel and the Arab countries; then he begins to feel pressures from "domestic considerations" which bend him and his colleagues toward policies other than those which the "estimates of the situation" would clearly dictate. Finally, he tries to devise solutions which make sense in the light of the intelligence estimates, and which can be justified by explanations which have no relation to the estimate but which accommodate to the domestic considerations.

For example:

1. Our intelligence estimators present frightening information concerning the Soviet build-up in Egypt, the increasing Soviet "presence" in the whole Mediterranean area, and the gains of Soviet naval strength east of Suez at the expense of the British. At the same time, they suggest, first, that Soviet gains have not been the result of Soviet actions, but of ours. The more we support Israel, the more the Arabs and their Afro-Asian friends welcome the Soviets. Second, the Soviet build-up is not in preparation for conquest—the Soviets would hardly try to gain by fighting what they can gain peacefully.

2. Daily, policy makers of the State Department read newspaper accounts of hawkish statements of Arab leaders: Syria's President proclaims loudly that his Government will "never" accept the existence of Israel; Iraq's President bitterly attacks Egypt's President for "defeatist tendencies," even though the speech in which the Egyptian is supposed to have shown such tendencies explicitly threatened war unless Israel withdrew "from every inch of Arab territory." And as our diplomats read such accounts they are aware that these are also being read by American opinion makers who take them at face value. At the same time, they know from the Department's own information that the most belligerent sounding Arab governments have in effect made peace with Israel already; such military preparations as these governments are making are strictly for internal purposes.

3. Our own press plays up the Soviet build-up in Egypt, and reports that "hot-headed young officers" are anxious for another round with Israel. Yet our State Department, depending not only on its highly competent diplomatic staff in Cairo but also on information coming from decades-old intelligence penetrations of the Egyptian armed forces, knows full well that Egyptian officers are possibly "fascist" but certainly not Communist, that they have little confidence in Soviet military assistance and don't like their Soviet advisers any more than the Turks and the Iranians like American advisers, that they are ready to fight for Egypt but not for Palestine or for "the Arabs," and that without the irritating presence of the Israelis in Sinai they would lack the motivation or morale to fight anyone at all.

4. Finally, our State Department officials know that Israeli intelligence estimates are roughly the same as our own. Thus, it is inconceivable that Israeli spokesmen could be sincere when they argue that qualified support to Israel is the only way to halt the growth of Soviet influence in the area, that they are in constant dread of being overrun by the Arabs, and that they must hold on to Sharm el-Sheik as a means of insuring passage through the Strait of Tiran. The Israelis know very well that they can take Sharm el-Sheik any time they wish, no matter who occupies it, and that their presence there will only provoke revival of Egyptian hostilities.

The Egyptians, seeing the Israelis' reluctance to seize this unique opportunity to make peace, suspect that they want a no-war-no-peace situation such as Nasser once wanted, and for similar (domestic) reasons. Apparently some of our NATO friends share the suspicion; so, increasingly, do some of our own diplomats. For good or for bad, right or wrong, and whatever the ultimate effect on purely American interests, we are behind the Israelis one hundred per cent. But we must make our own policy in Washington and not let the Israelis make it for us in Tel Aviv. If domestic considerations stand

Death as Precept

Fons van Woerkom

By TAKESHI MURAMATSU

TOKYO — In the Christian world, suicide is considered a grave sin. But for Japanese people, it carries a significance unknown to Christendom. In certain cases, suicide can be an extremely beautiful act, worthy of the highest praise.

On Nov. 25 of last year, Yukio Mishima, one of Japan's most famous writers, committed suicide by *seppuku*. Here, it is important to state that he did not commit suicide because he had failed in a *coup*. Mishima's purpose, in sight from the first, was to perform *seppuku*. It was because of this that he went to the Eastern District Headquarters of the Self-Defense Force and had the soldiers assembled before he died. He tried to explain what he intended to do and then killed himself, as he had arranged beforehand. All the evidence shows that he was not attempting a *coup d'état* and that even the police did not consider it as anything other than a suicide.

From 1967 on, Mishima was strug-

As a basis for the revival of traditional spirit, he put his hopes in the army. However, it was not the body of "samurai" that he envisaged. Mishima then despaired, but he determined to remonstrate with the army and the people by killing himself. It was intended as a "death as precept."

Since ancient times, the Japanese have been a people who attach great importance to a beautiful death. The "Tale of Genji," written early in the eleventh century, repeatedly glorifies a "pure" death, a death which is not obsessed with the things of this world. In the thirteenth-century epic romance, "The Tale of the Heike," the warrior was one who accepted death willingly when he realized it was a fate from which he could not escape.

In the Christian world, one's life could be shortened only as the Lord pleased, and therefore suicide was a heresy to God. But to the Japanese, death was the point at which each person made contact with the eternal

It is difficult to summarize Mishima's vast literary output, but it can be said that the heart of his esthetic is that the ecstatic burning of human passion once in a lifetime is what gives life its meaning. On the other hand, he was aware that this belief could be an illusion. This was his paradox as a modern writer. On the same day he wrote the last chapter of "The Sea of Fertility," a work that suggested that all was illusion, he took a Japanese sword in his hand and went to the place of *seppuku*, where his flame was to burn for all eternity.

The impact of his death on the Japanese people was very great. To say the least, it was the greatest psychological shock since World War II.

His death brought forth all kinds of criticism. Although it did not cause either left or right to reappraise their ideologies, the hearts of Japanese were deeply stained. Since the Second World War, they had been solely occupied with building an affluent society, but as a result of Mishima's suicide, the

THE THIRD SECTION, "FACE TO FACE," IS A KIND OF CHRONICLE OF POLITICAL AND SOCIAL EVENTS. IT PRESENTED A GREAT OPPORTUNITY TO COMMENT AND TO VISUALIZE MY OWN STATEMENT, WHOSE IMPORTANCE LIES IN ITS ABILITY TO CONFRONT MYSELF AND OTHERS WITH OUR LIMITATIONS.—FONS VAN WOERKOM

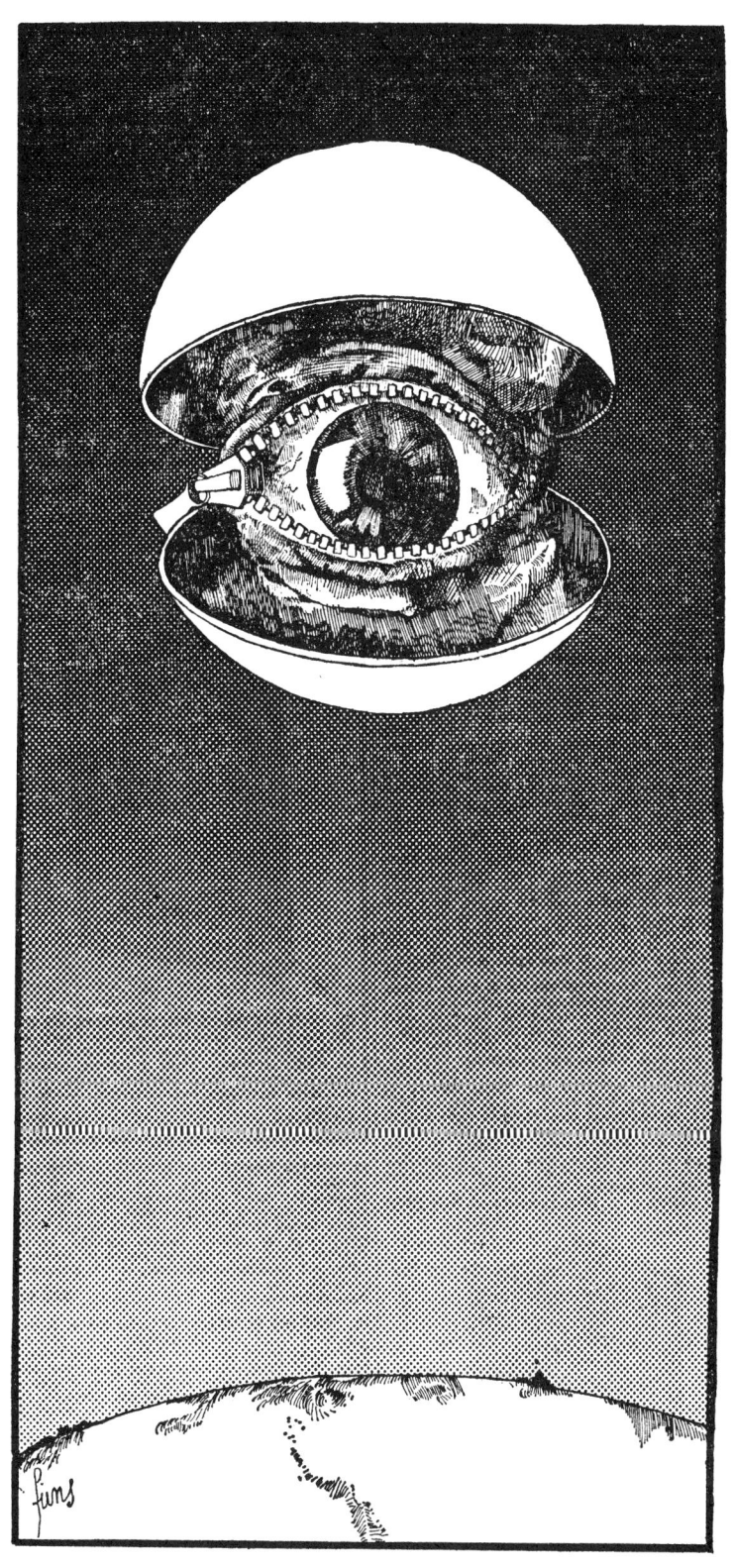

REOPEN THE SKIES

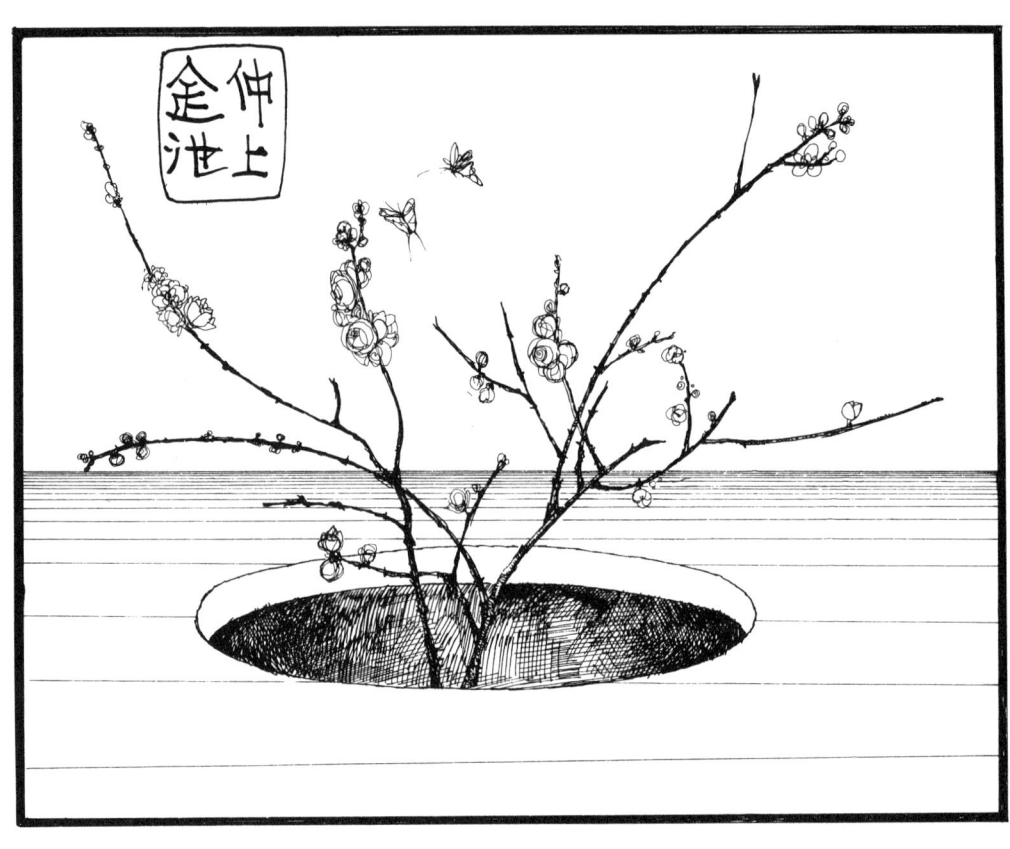

JAPAN BEFORE WORLD WAR II

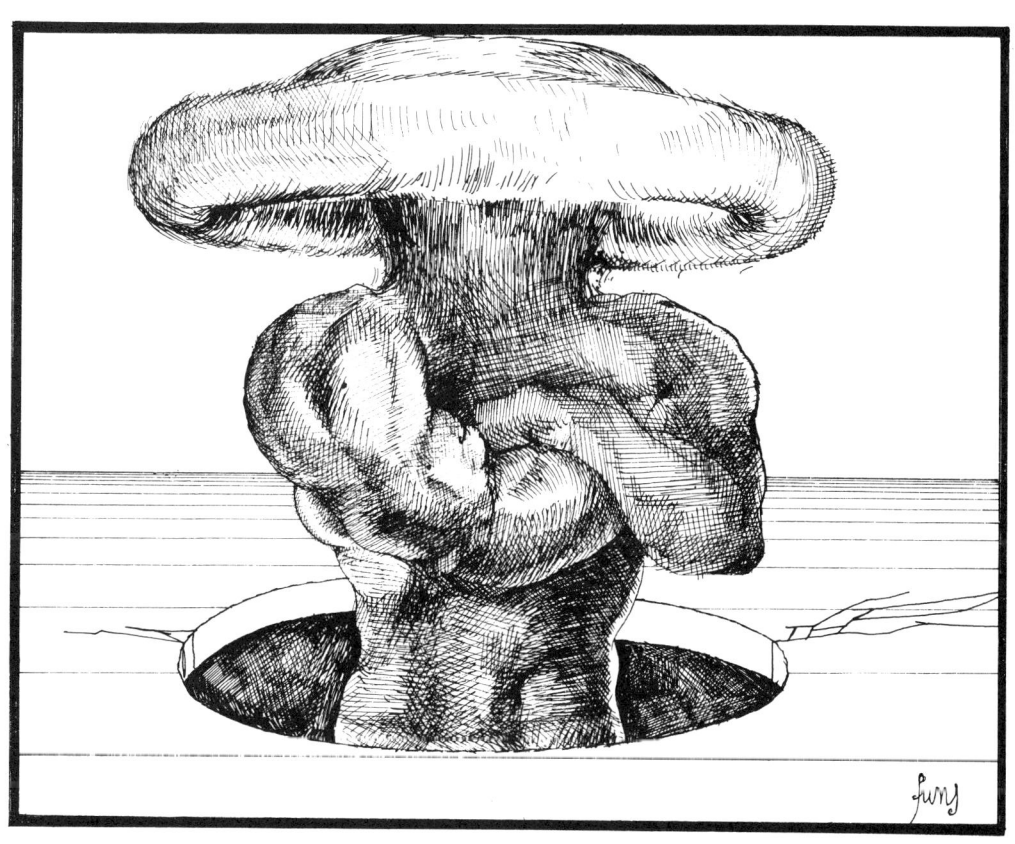

...AFTER

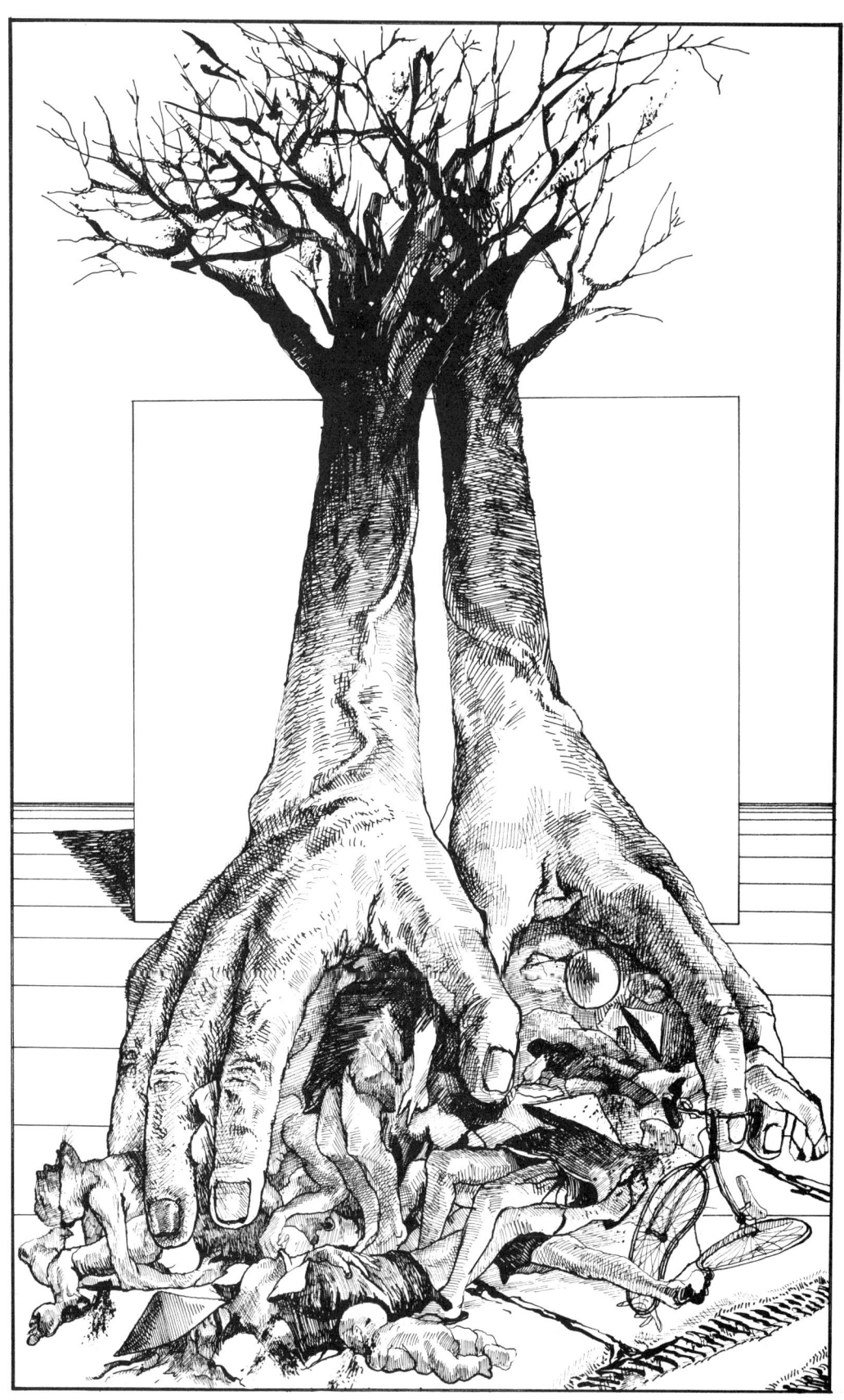

MY LAI...AFTERMATH

NORMAN MAILER   "FIRE ON THE MOON"

"PRISONER OF SEX"

SCOOP FOR GREED

DEFEAT WITH HONOR

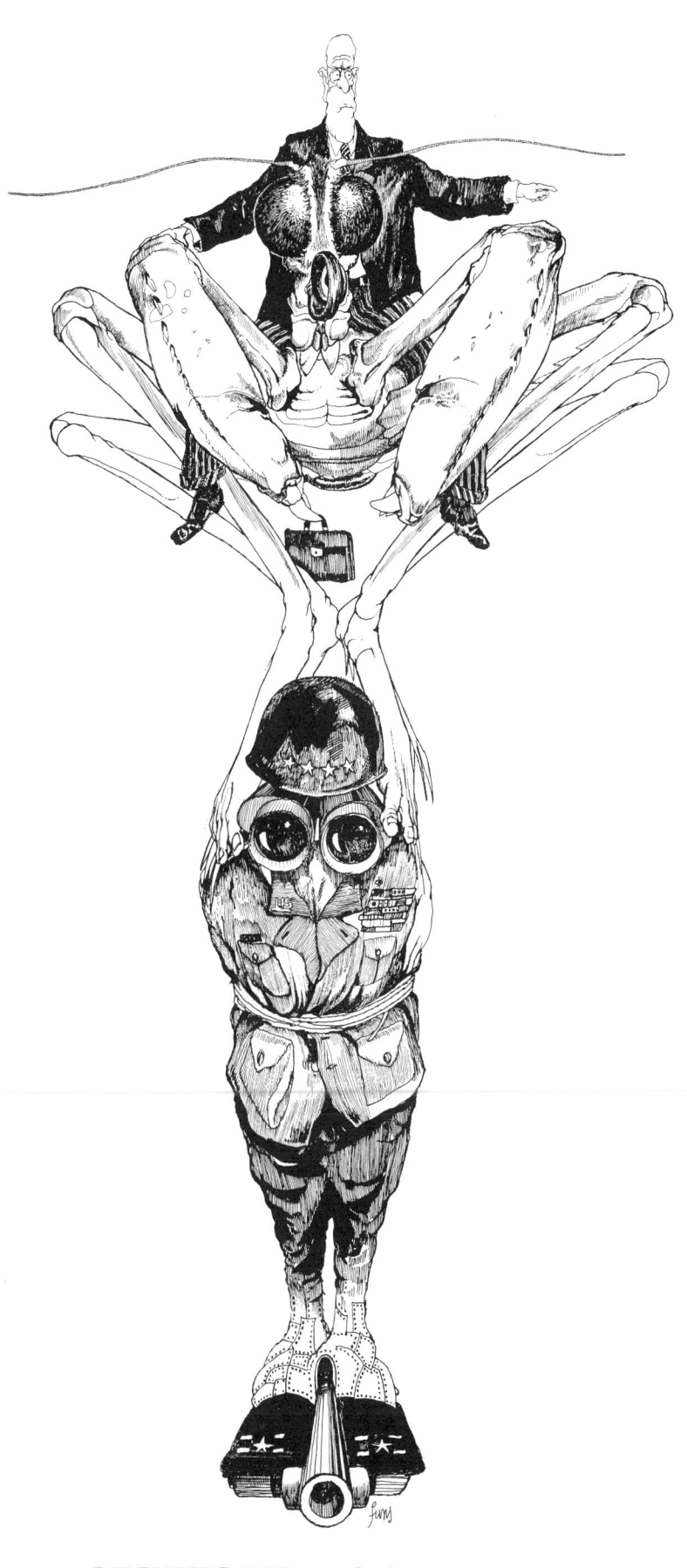

LEAVING WAR TO CIVILIANS

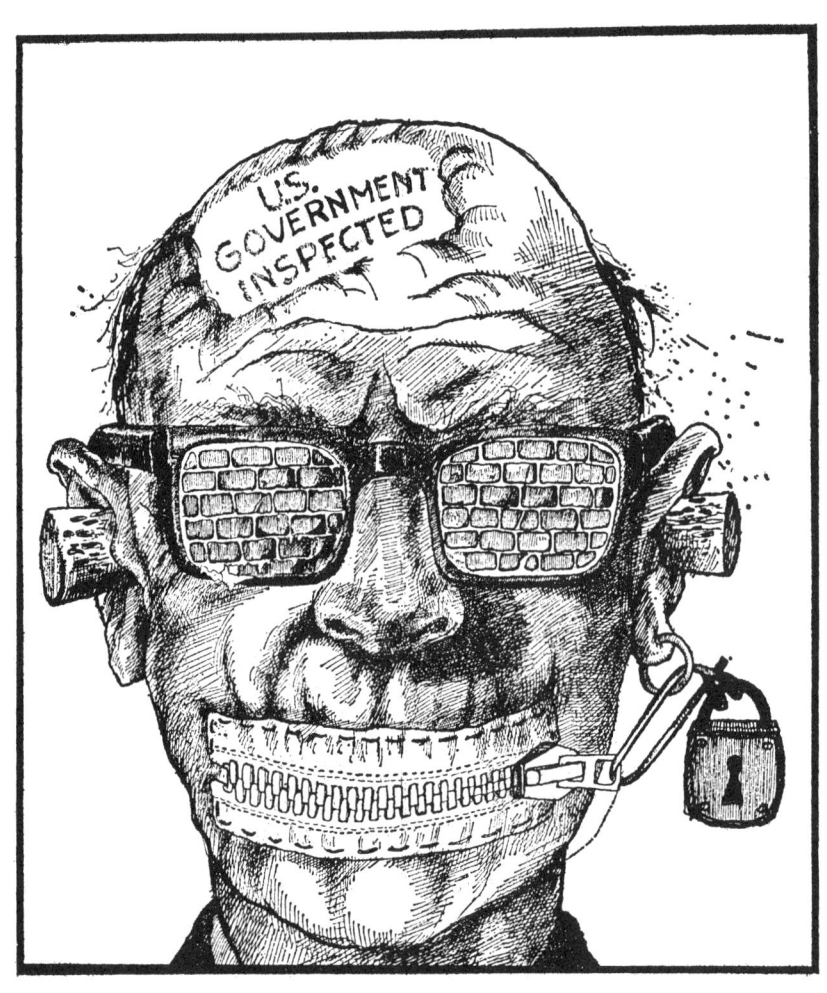

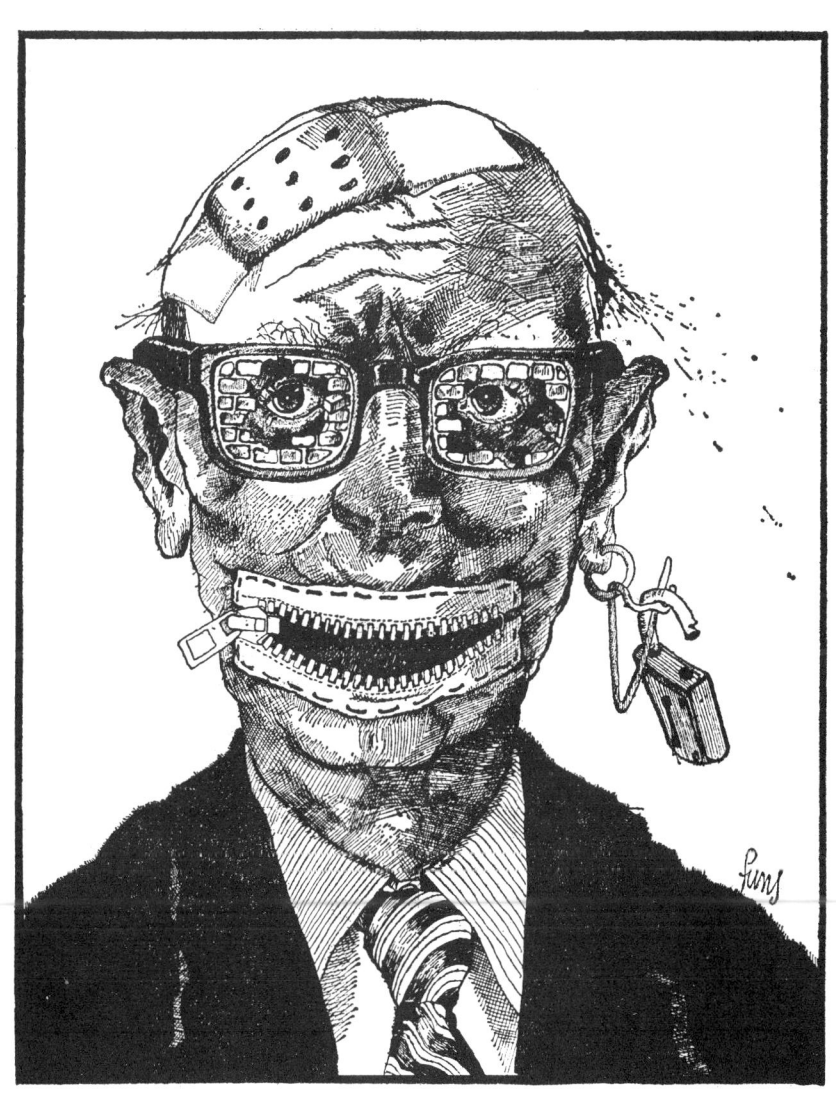

KAFKA AND THE NEWS

THE MILITARY AND MORALITY

STEPS TOWARD VIETNAMIZATION

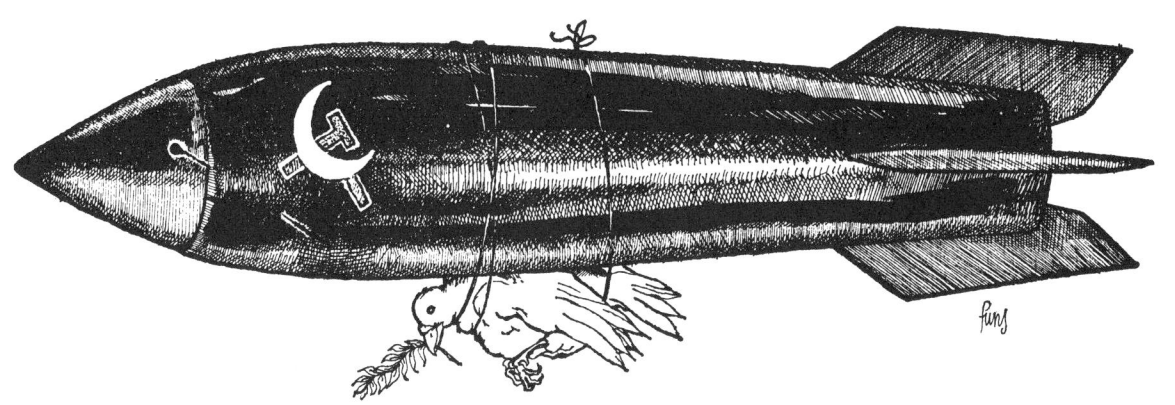

MIDDLE EAST: NEW WINGS OF THE DOVE

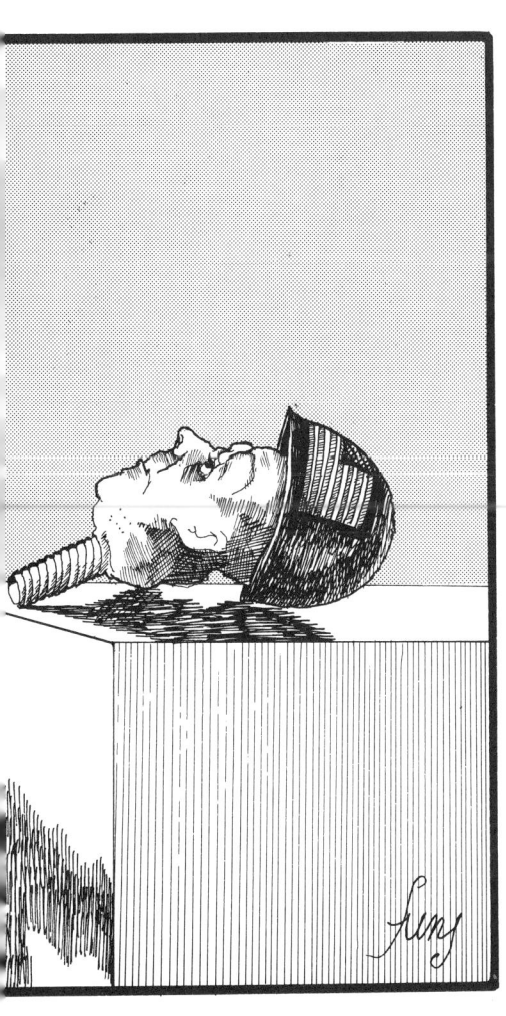

DEATH AS PRECEPT

MACMILLAN RECALLS

"YOU DON'T GET ME TWICE." JOHN LENNON

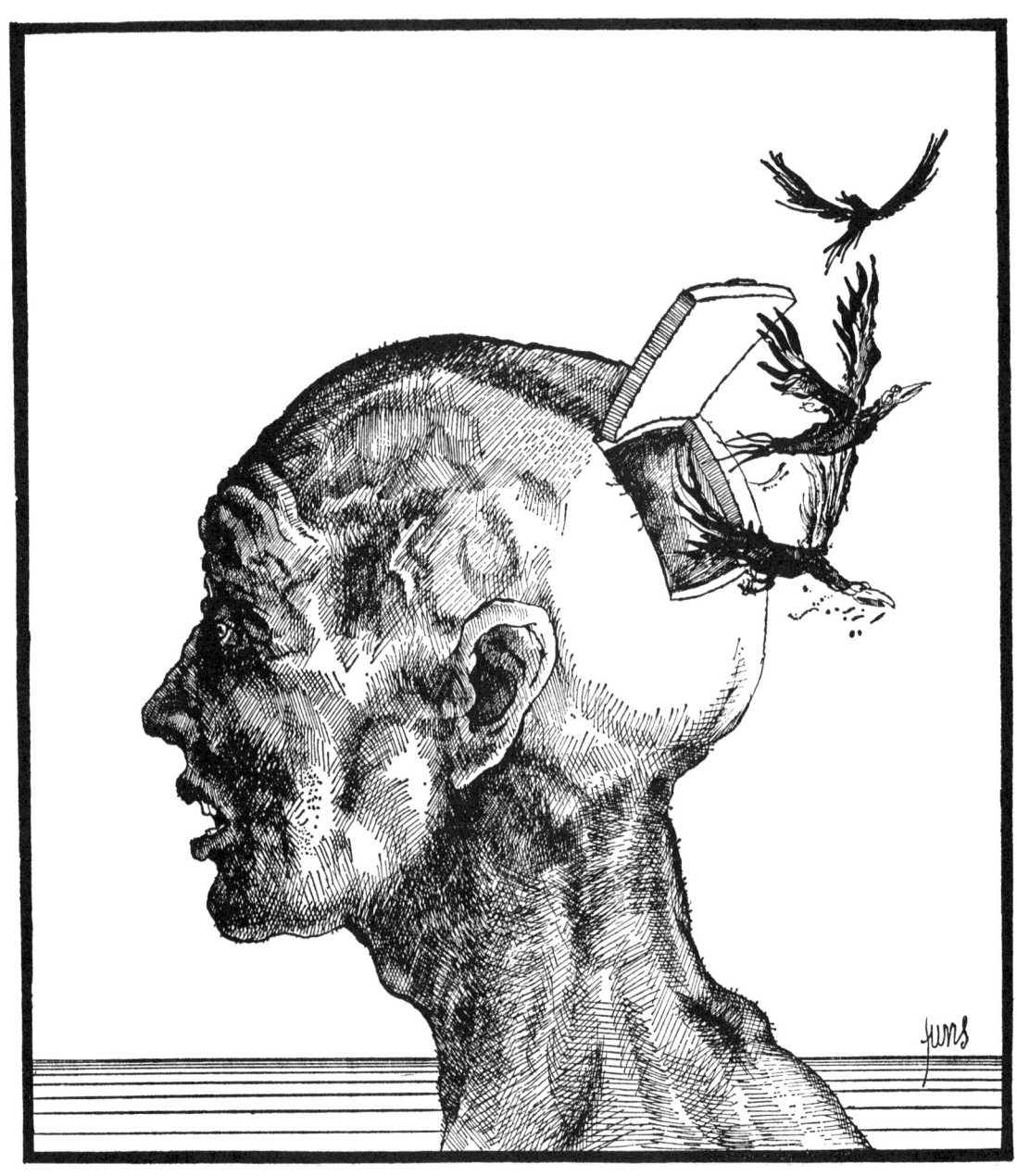

DEPRESSION

"THINK RHINOCEROS OR ALL IS LOST"

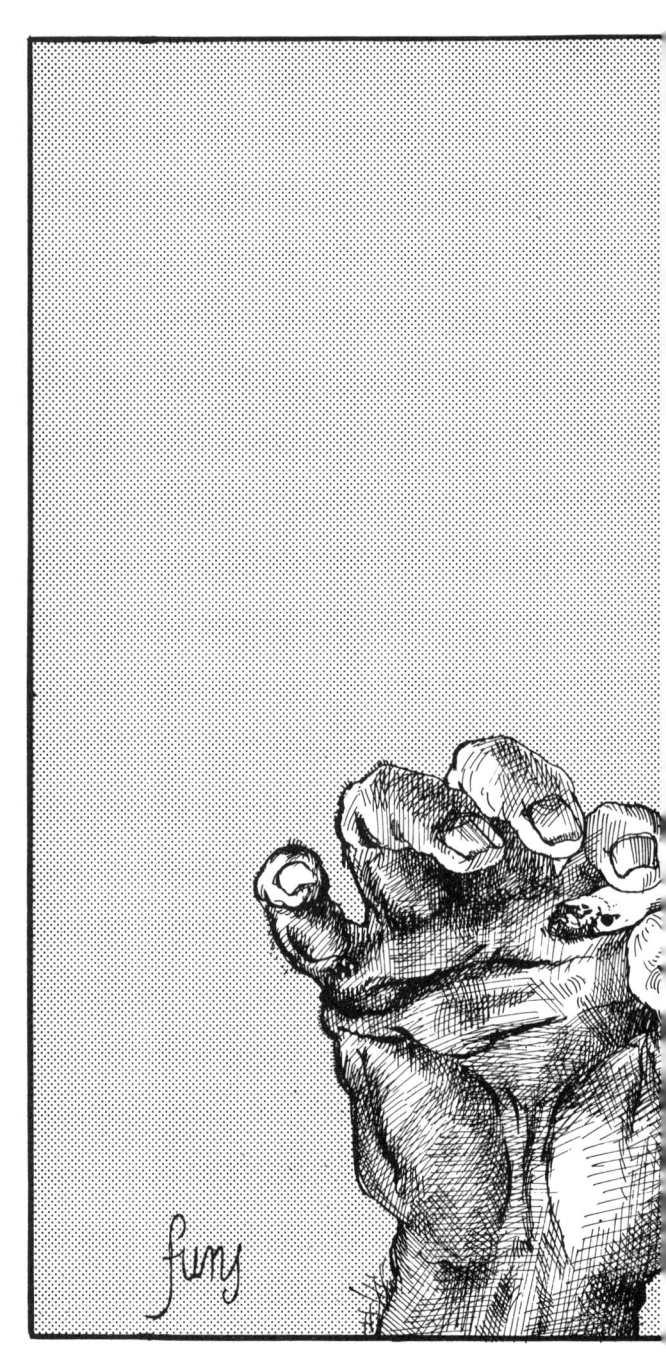

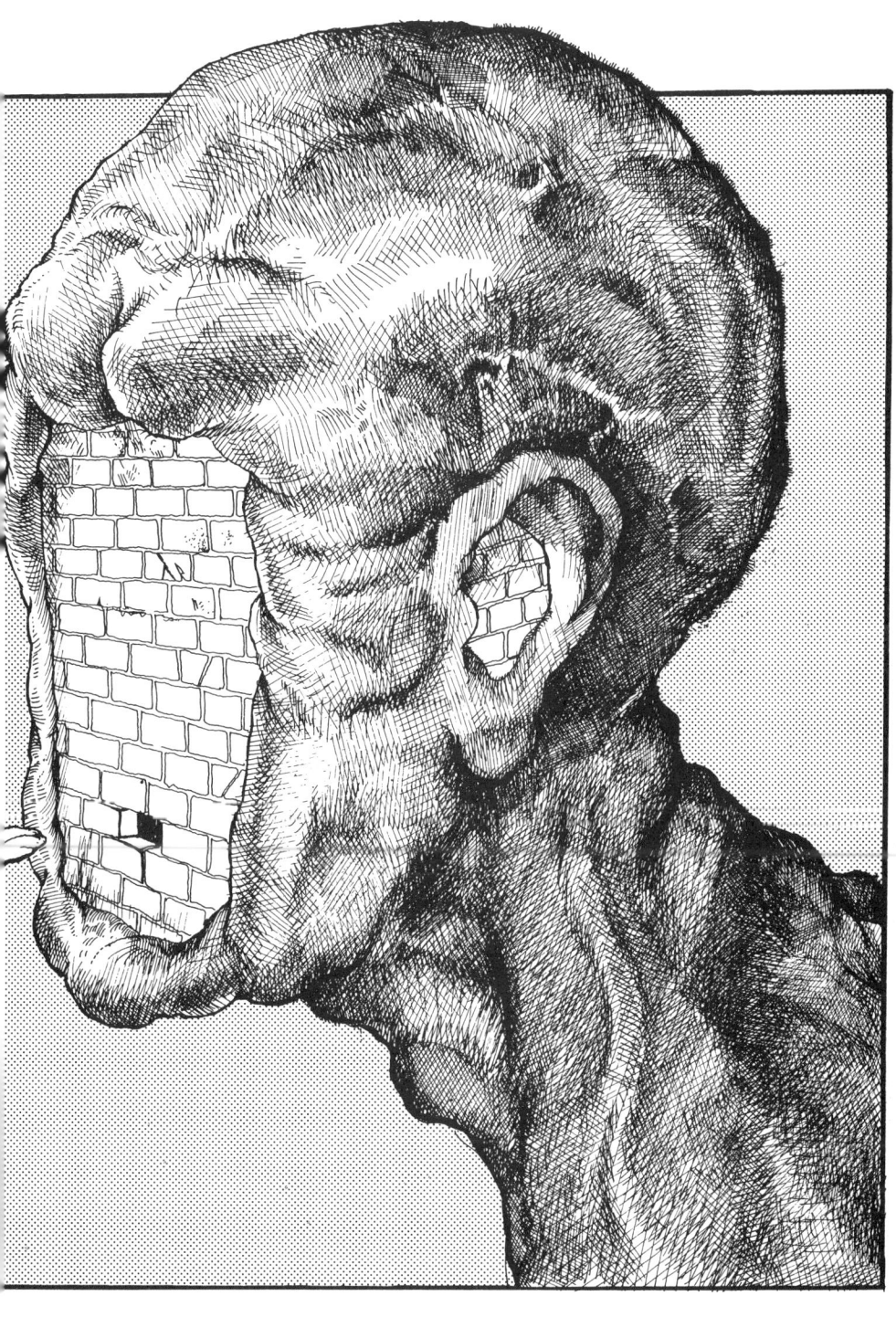

MARIJUANA: PRO OR CON

**WILLIAM BUCKLEY
A SPLIT IN THE RIGHT WING**

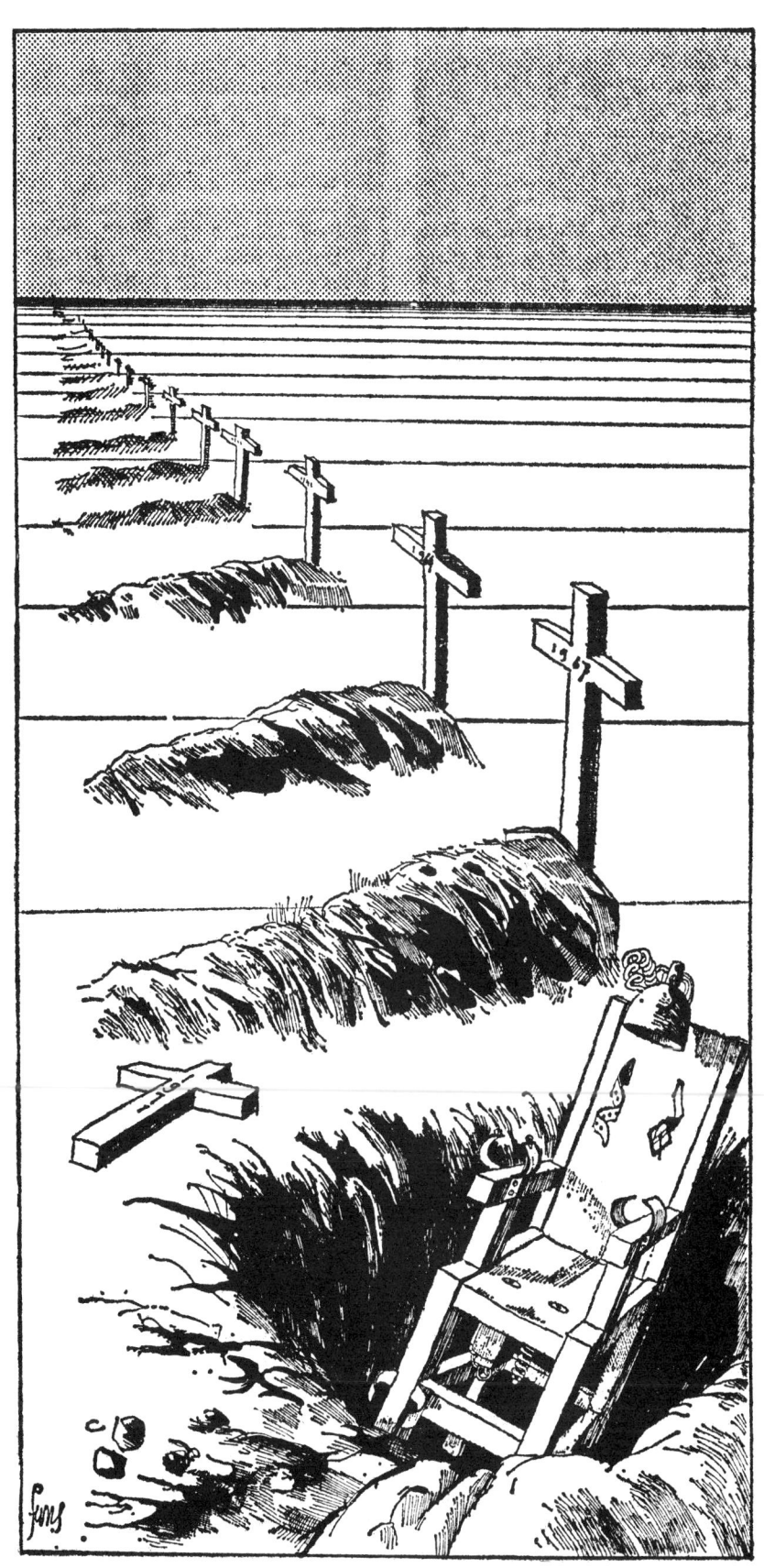

REQUIEM IN PACE

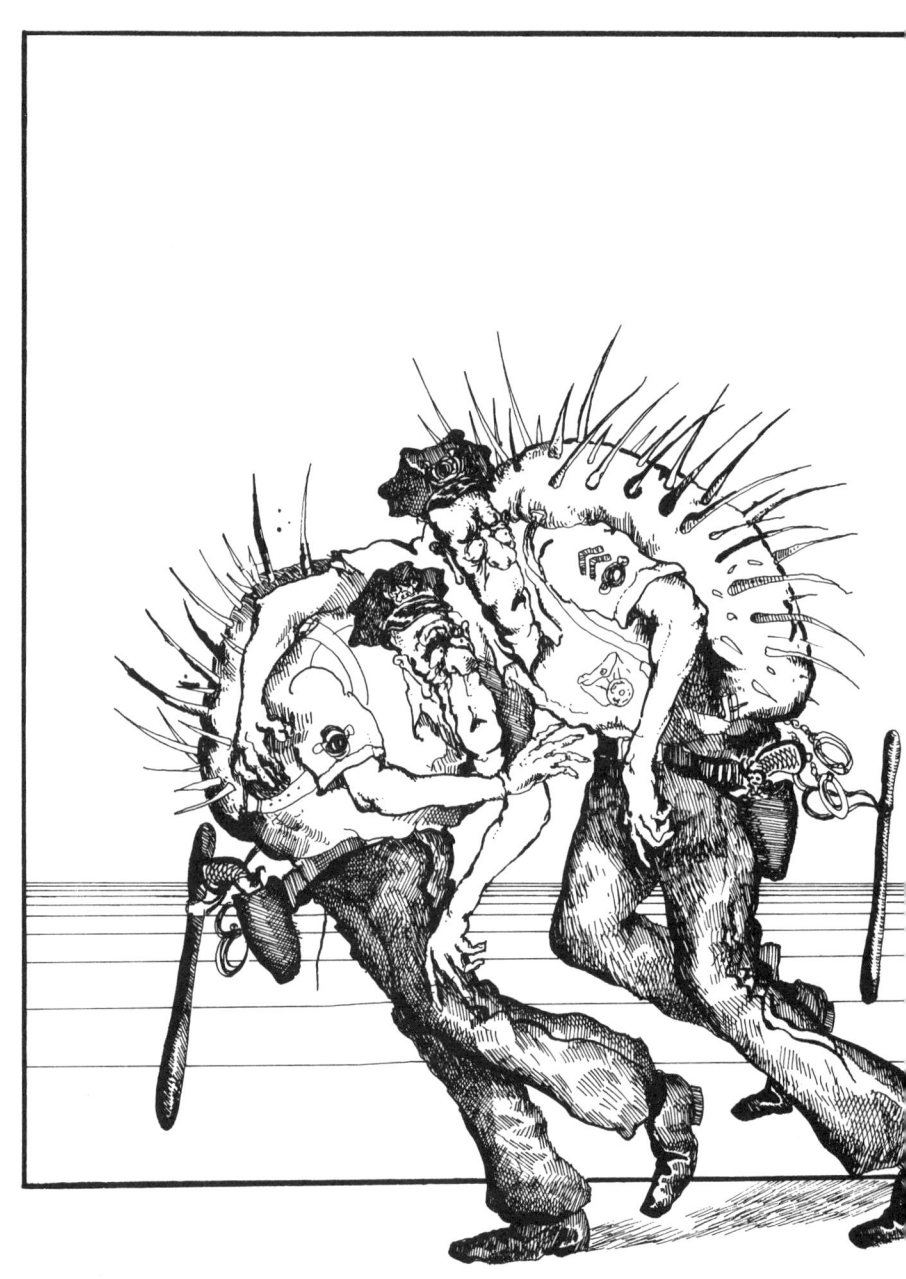

VIOLENCE AND POLICE

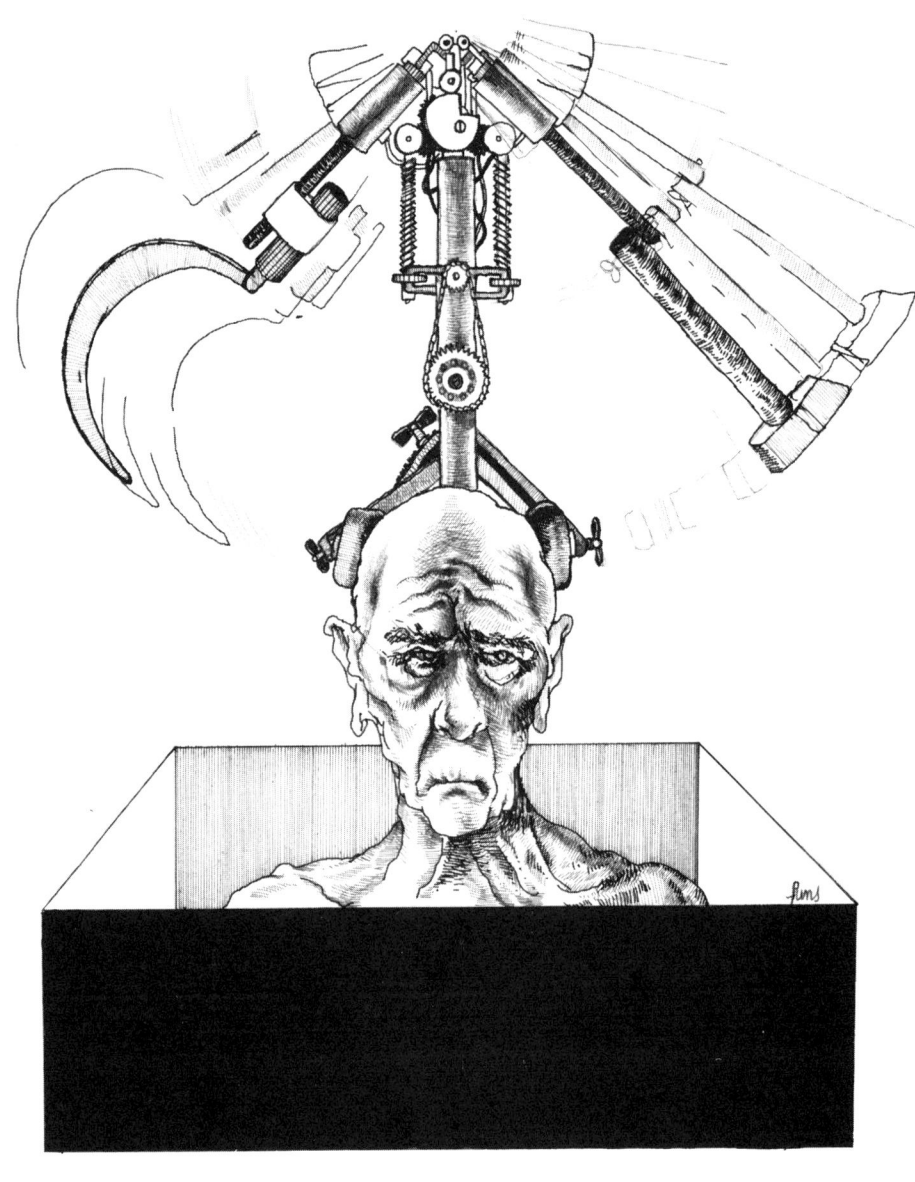

"A QUESTION OF MADNESS"

THE MILITANT BLUECOATS

GENERAL MATTHEW B. RIDGWAY

BEHIND THE UNIFORM

THE GREAT SOCIETY

THE WISDOM OF EISENHOWER

"ASK NOT..."

KING RAT

POLICE FRAME-UP UNCOVERED

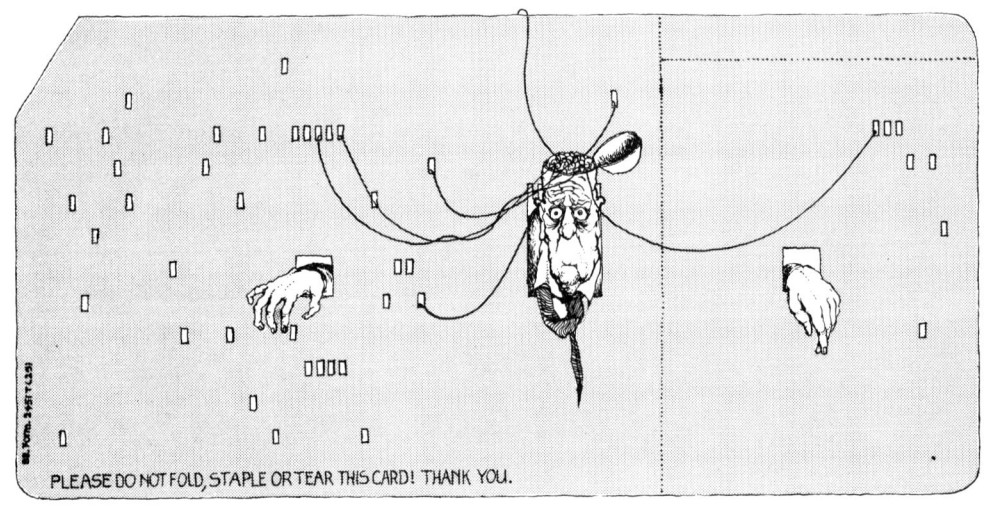

LOVE THAT CORPORATION

WE BECOME WHAT WE HATE

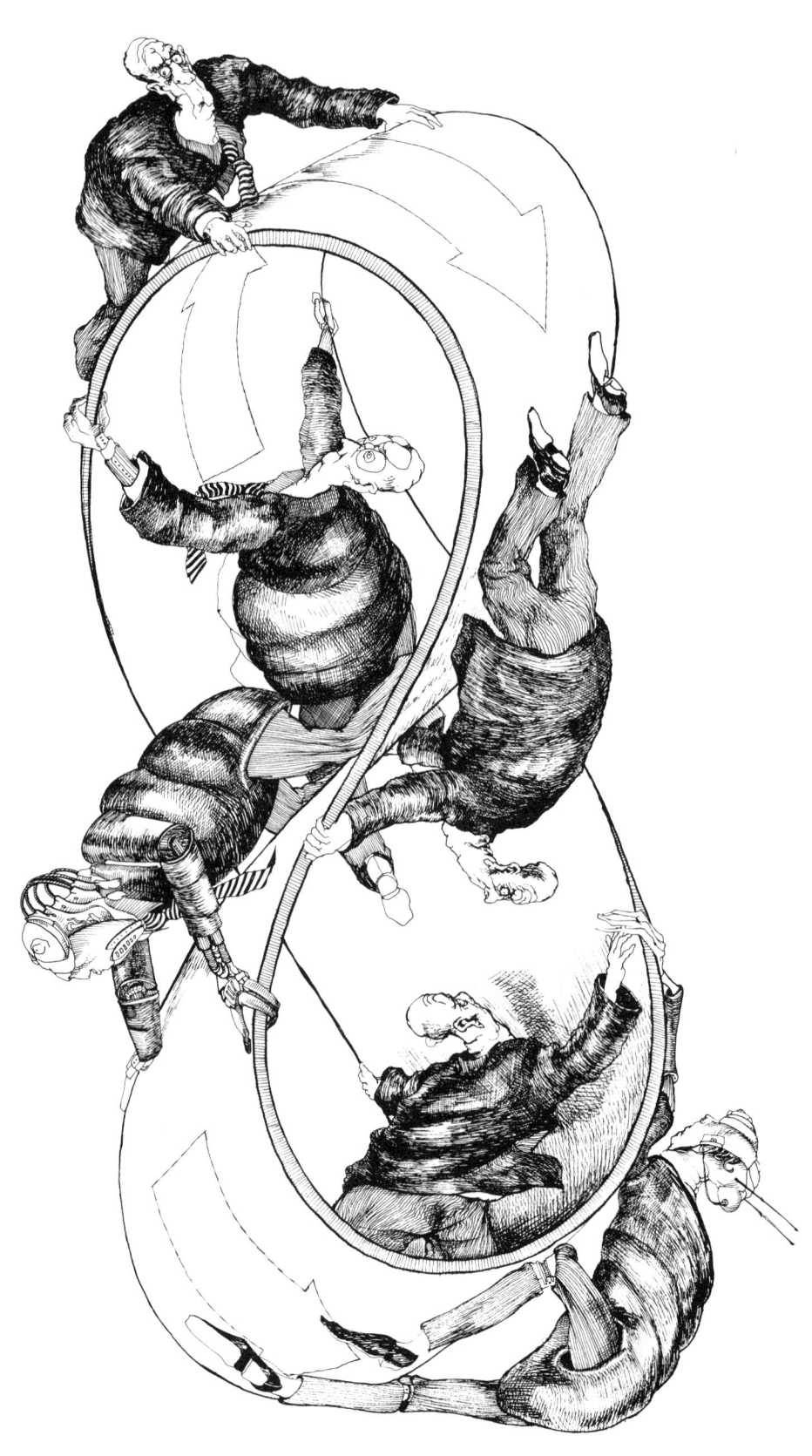

CAN BUCKMINSTER FULLER SAVE US?

THE BOMBING DECISION: THE MAN BEHIND

HOUSE COMMITTEE ON UN-AMERICAN ACTIVITIES

LOST CHINA

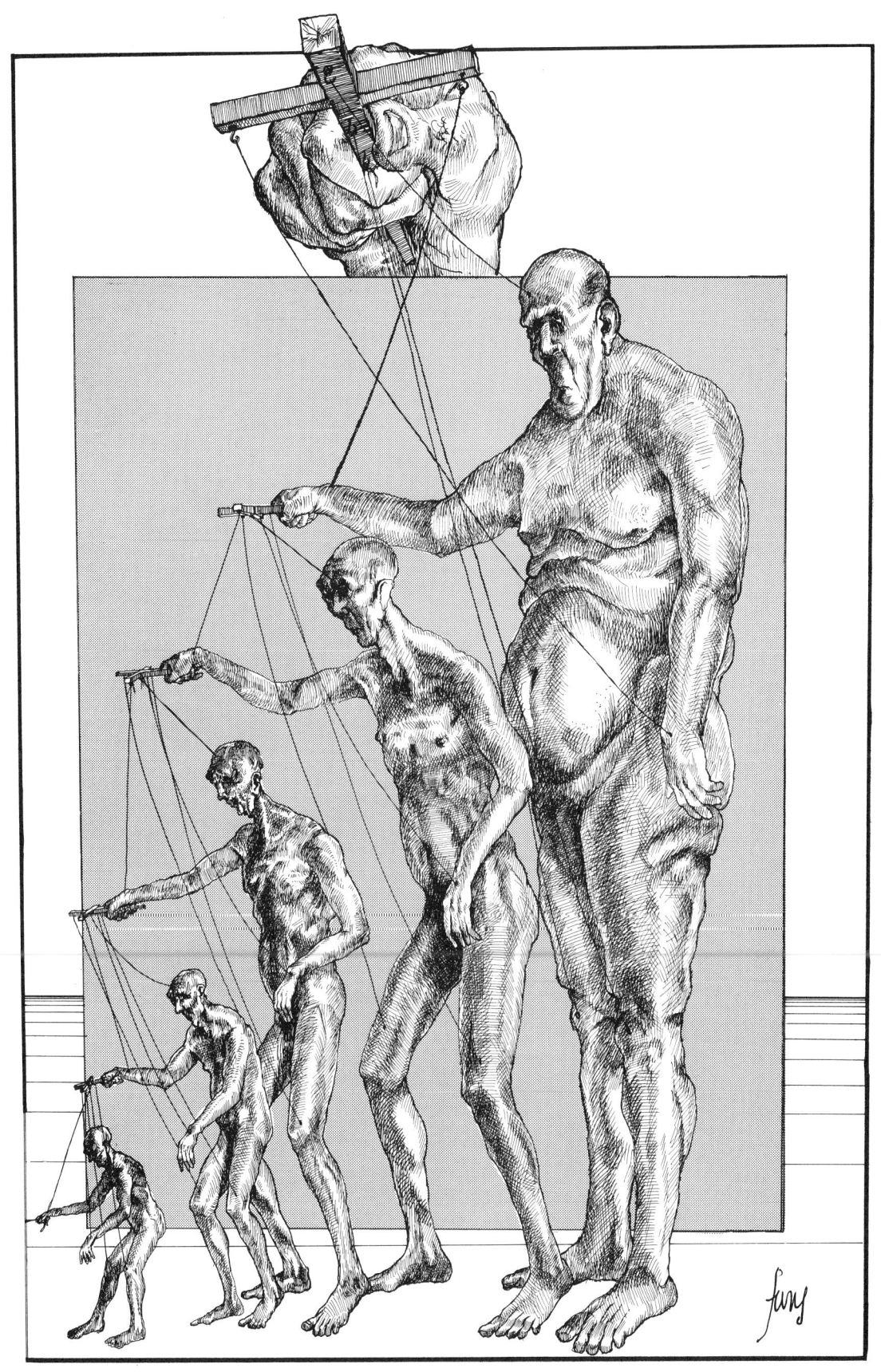

THE WATERGATE

ABOUT THE ARTIST

Fons van Woerkom, well-known for his *New York Times* illustrations, was born in Holland in 1943. He studied painting for eight years and graduated from the Jan van Eyck Academy in Maastricht, Holland. In 1968 he moved to Canada and worked as a free-lance political cartoonist for the Toronto *Daily Star*. Van Woerkom won the International Political Cartoon Award in 1970 and shortly afterward moved to New York, where he is currently living with his wife and two-year-old son.